AMERICAN TERRORIST
"A Grandfather's Revenge"

Book one in the series: American Terrorist

By

Ron L. Carter

***

Chapter 1 - Introduction

It was December 2, 2009, and Michael was up and ready to join his team at 0500 hours. It was a cold winter morning in Kunduz, Afghanistan, and patches of dark clouds were still in the sky from a light snowfall the day before. This mission was unlike all the other missions of the Special Force Team. Usually, missions don't just happen spontaneously; there is a lot of time planning to ensure they are successful. Almost all Special Forces missions occur at night and are done in total secrecy. This mission was on a convoy and during the daylight hours. Before the mission, meetings are held, briefings are given, and jobs are assigned. Accountability of assets, personnel, and intelligence is exchanged, and current conditions are analyzed to complete the mission.

As Michael headed out of the safe house to the convoy, he was excited but apprehensive as his body shivered from the cold Afghanistan air. He knew it wasn't just the cold air that made him shiver but maybe from fear of what lay ahead for him and his team.

On this mission, Michael's team worked alongside the Afghanistan Northern Alliance to set up a meeting with the village chief of Kharid-e Olya, who was just outside Kunduz. The Special Forces teams act as ambassadors, protectors, and instructors to the Afghans who desire to free themselves of the Taliban militants.

The village chief is one that Michael's team had been hoping to convince for a long time to accept the coalition forces' safety and protection. The Team aimed to bridge the villages to the United States led by the allied Federal Afghan Government. The chief had finally agreed to a meeting in the Village with Michael's team, and they were taking a convoy into the village.

The team also worked with the Afghan Uniformed Police, known as the Special Tactic Team, which consisted of Afghan soldiers with advanced training. Together, the units had found and cleared insurgent-buried bombs known as I.E.D. s (improvised explosive devices) in many different locations.

They went out before Michael's team was deployed, searched, and cleared the roads for I.E.D.s. They had tried everything possible to implement a safe passage for Michael's team. To add additional stress to the mission, Michael's team had recently found that a local commander normally allied with the United States military was betraying American intentions and foiling operations to capture Taliban and al-Qaeda soldiers. (18)

The convoy had four Humvees; each consisted of a fire team: fire team leader, vehicle driver, and a gunner. When the convoy starts moving or is in a fixed position, a 360-degree perimeter of security is always maintained.

Everything was quiet and normal for the first several miles, but as the convoy got within a few miles of the village, they started receiving incoming small-arms fire on both sides of the road. The enemy insurgents were hiding approximately two hundred yards away, and it was hard to know their exact location. The convoy immediately came to a halt, and the gunners on the Humvees sent out suppressing fire in a spray pattern.

The exchange of gunfire lasted about eight minutes, and then it stopped as quickly as it had begun. The incoming rounds hit none of the American forces, but it was still slightly intimidating.

The convoy slowly started to move and only went another forty yards when a large I.E.D. hit Michael's Humvee. He was thrown about fifteen feet from the Humvee upon the explosion's impact. He immediately lost consciousness, and when he woke up, he was in excruciating pain, and his legs were mangled from the explosion. His left leg was missing from the thigh, and his left arm was from the elbow.

He could hear a team member yelling and calling for a medevac. When he saw the damage to himself, he knew he would be dead within a few minutes. His first reaction was to crawl to the destroyed Humvee and find his medical kit. He soon found it was no use; he could only get a few feet before starting to blackout again.

Michael could hear some team members crying in pain as they yelled for medical help. He was the medical sergeant, and now he was one of the ones that needed help. Once the Humvee blew up, the enemy insurgents started firing on the convoy with heavy small arms fire. The convoy was pinned down, and he knew that help would be too late as he lost consciousness again.

When one of his team members finally arrived, he vigorously shook Michael to see if he was still alive. For a moment, he woke up and opened his eyes. It was just long enough to see it was one of his best friends from his team. Just before he took his last breath, he said, "Tell my grandpa I love him."

Grief is horrible; it can humble, devastate, or destroy you. There is no more profound pain than a father or mother having to bury one of their children. The devastating news destroyed Doug when he found out about Michael.

***

Chapter 2 - The Early Years

Doug and Shirley had raised Michael since he was two and a half years after the fatal car accident that killed their daughter and husband. Doug felt more like a father to Michael than a grandfather. His grief was almost unbearable when Michael was killed in Afghanistan.

When Michael was killed in Afghanistan at the hands of the militant terrorist insurgents, Doug felt he had nothing else to live for. He had lost his only daughter and son-in-law in a car accident when they were young, and his wife, Shirley, had died of cancer a few years earlier.

The love and compassion Doug once had for all people were replaced with anger and hatred toward the radical Muslim terrorist organizations for what they had done to Michael. Because of his deep-seated hatred, he declared his war of vengeance against their organizations in America. Michael's last words were forever haunting him.

The military officials told Dr. Doug James Cotton that he was fighting to stop the militant terrorist insurgents from spreading their jihad to America at Michael's death. The Military said Michael helped stop global terrorism by destroying the terrorist training camps in Afghanistan and making peace with the local leaders.

Afghanistan was home to the militant terrorist organization known as al-Qaeda. Doug was very familiar with warfare because of his fighting in South Vietnam in 1968 (during the Tet Offensive). He had seen firsthand the death and destruction of war and, as a sniper, had killed countless North Vietnam and Viet Cong Soldiers during his tour of duty.

He had done extensive research on the radical terrorist organizations when Michael was in the military and knew they already had terrorist cells in America, poised and ready to attack command. During his months of research, Doug was utterly shocked to find over thirty-five known radical Muslim Jihad terrorist sleeper cells in twenty-two United States states. They hide under the disguise of many types of organizations in America. They exploit the United States Constitution (freedom of speech, assembly, and religion) as their shield to carry out their destructive goals of terrorism.

Once Michael was in the military and committed to fighting the radical militant terrorists, Doug's goal was to find out everything he could about the terrorists and how their organizations worked. He read and studied the Qur'an (Islam's holy book) and the basis for the Muslim religion. He studied everything he could about the radical militant Muslim extremist (the terrorist). He took a home study course, learned Arabic, Urdu, and Farsi languages, and became proficient. He learned everything he could about their way of life. He studied how the Muslims prayed, dressed, their mannerisms, and customs. He also studied and learned about Kabul and Kandahar in Afghanistan and other towns in Iraq people.

Douglas Cotton was born in the San Joaquin Valley town of Visalia, California, on January 28, 1949. When Doug grew up in Visalia during the fifties and early sixties, the town had approximately eleven thousand people. Since then, it has grown to over one hundred and twenty-five thousand.

His childhood was expected, and like most kids of that time, most of his free time growing up was spent helping his father on the farm he had to help his father on the farm. His mother and father owned a nice older farmhouse with a hundred-and-sixty-acre walnut grove a few miles from town. He loved living on the farm but didn't want to do farm work as a profession for the rest of his life. Much to his father's disappointment, Doug wanted to do something different with his life when he grew up.

Doug's Brother Randy was seven years younger and was just the opposite of him. He had sandy-colored hair and was a few inches shorter and heavier than Doug. They didn't have a real close relationship because of the age difference. He loved Randy, but they didn't have that much in common. Doug felt that Randy was always poking his nose into his business, where he didn't belong. Doug didn't share many of his opinions and ideas with him.

When Doug was a junior in high school, he was six feet tall with dark brown wavy hair and brown eyes. He was always well-groomed and not a hair out of place. He weighed about one hundred and seventy pounds but had many wiry, stiff muscles. He was a good athlete and lettered in his junior and senior high school years on the varsity football and basketball teams.

He dated a few girls in high school, but none interested him until he met Shirley Stevens in his junior year. He had seen her at school and was attracted to her but didn't think she was interested in him, so he never tried to meet her.

Shirley was five feet six inches tall and thin, with dark brown hair and dimples on her cheeks when she smiled. After Shirley's accident, they started dating and were inseparable. Although Shirley was in the same school year as Doug, she was more mature than most girls her age. It seemed to him that she was ready to settle down and get married after the first several dates. He didn't have a problem because he had fallen for her. They both just knew right from the beginning that someday they would end up married to each other.

After dating for over a year and a few weeks before they graduated from high school, Shirley gave him the news that he would be a father. That news would change both their lives forever. Shirley was about two months into her pregnancy when they married in June. Doug went to work for his father on the family farm but knew it would only be temporary.

* * *

Chapter 3 – Doug's Drafted into the Army

The Vietnam War was in full swing and ever-present in the news and on everyone's mind, especially young men of Doug's age. He was classified by the military as 1A when he turned eighteen and registered with the draft board. The army was drafting every available young man who wasn't attending college, which could qualify as 1A. You couldn't fight the draft unless you had a school deferment or had a 4F (physical condition) that kept you out. You had to spend a mandatory two-year term in the military once drafted.

Not long after Doug was out of school, he received the dreaded notice that he had been drafted into the United States Army. Since he worked full-time and wasn't attending college, he had no way to fight the draft. He would have to leave Shirley at home to have the baby without him. Shirley was already in her sixth month when he left for basic training. They agreed she would move back home with her parents until his stint with the military was over or at least until his duty station was close to home where they could live together.

Once drafted, they sent him to Fort Benning, Georgia, for his nine weeks of basic training and then to Fort Polk, Louisiana, for his nine weeks of advanced training. There were a lot of letters written back and forth to Shirley, and he received a letter from her almost daily. While training, he discovered he was an expert marksman with a them-14 rifle, hitting ninety-eight percent of his targets from over three hundred yards.

The Army decided they wanted to make a sniper out of him, so after basic and advanced training, they sent him through sniper school for four weeks. After training, the Army gave him a thirty-day leave of absence to go home before going to Vietnam.

Doug had been in the military for five and a half months, and when he got home on leave, he finally met his beautiful baby girl. Before he left for the Army, they decided they would name her Jenifer if they had a girl. For the first few days, he was home. He just sat around, held her, cuddled her, and admired her beauty. He was so excited about being a father; he thought it was the best thing ever happening to him besides meeting Shirley.

He spent some great days at home but felt it was not long enough before he had to leave. He was worried and excited about what lay ahead in South Vietnam the entire time he was home. Then the day came, and he was on his way to the jungles of Vietnam.

He was sent to Dong Tam Sniper Headquarters when he arrived in Vietnam. Once there, they briefed him and told him where he would be stationed and what his mission was in Vietnam. His permanent duty station in Vietnam was at Tiger Lair. He had been trained in the XM-21 - M-14 rifle with a 3 X 9 Redfield Scope. This rifle was good for several hundred yards. He also trained in the XM -21 M-14 rifle with a silencer (good only up to about three hundred yards but great against the Viet Cong). He received both rifles once he arrived at Dong Tam. (1)

The Viet Cong were villagers and other local people already in the country that was fighting alongside the North Vietnamese soldiers. The (VC) and the North Vietnamese soldiers were small and elusive targets, with an average of five foot three to five foot five inches tall. They almost always wore silky black tops and silky black loose-fitting pajama-looking pants. The North Vietnamese soldiers were different, having full uniforms and military-issued boots.

Doug spent much of his time being sent to locations where the V.C. had been spotted. He was called to go in and kill the enemy. Because of the enemy's distance, he never looked at them as "people" when he shot them. They were just "targets" to him. If he didn't take out his targets, they would just set up an ambush somewhere in the jungle and kill his friends.

About three days a month, Doug was sent out on the Army's Mobile Riverine Forge in the Mekong Delta to scout out and kill the VC that may be waiting in ambush along the river as United States military personnel went by. Sometimes, they would briefly encounter the VC, but the VC would disappear when they received an incoming fire in their positions. Those days seemed like a break from the lonely and tedious life back at base camp, where he waited for the call to go to a specific area and shoot the enemy. Many of his days were uneventful, slow, and tedious because no VC was spotted. Doug learned how to play Cribbage with his friends, and they also played a lot of poker during that time.

On one of his missions, he was told by his commanding officer that he and one of his fellow snipers, Calvin Yates, would be dropped off in the jungle where the VC had been spotted. Calvin was a nice guy but a little too boisterous for Doug's taste. He was from the south and had a twang in his voice. Whenever he killed a VC or North Vietnamese soldier, he would yell, "How'd you like them apples, you miserable little gook." He was always bragging about the body count. Calvin was excited about getting more bodies to count, but Doug hoped to come back alive and not be injured.

They were put on the helicopter and flown deep into the jungle about twenty-five miles from his base camp. There was nothing around but thick brush and trees. When they arrived, an open area was big enough to land the chopper. They called it the (landing zone) or LZ.

As they were dropped off, the pilot told them he would return to pick them up before dark, around 1800 hours. Little did Doug know then, but the VC had also spotted the helicopter and knew where it had touched down. Once they were on the ground, the VC was on their hunt to find the two of them.

They headed for the trees to find cover as soon as they got off the helicopter. They needed to find an observation point to get a good idea of the VC's location. Doug and Yates decided to split up to cover more areas, and they made plans to meet back at the LZ before it was time to be picked up. The jungle was so thick there weren't any clear enemy routes or trails. After about an hour of creeping through the jungle, he found a location where he felt he could spot the VC if they crossed an open area about three hundred yards away.

After fighting the mosquitoes and other insects for forty-five minutes, Doug spotted five VC groups crossing his target area. He took careful aim with his rifle and scope and squeezed off a round, taking out one of his targets. He then quickly aimed and soon had another one taken out. Before he could kill more of them, the remaining soldiers pulled their wounded friends into the heavy trees and disappeared. He waited a few minutes to see if they would reappear, but they didn't.

From experience, he knew he had to move quickly to another location because they would locate his position and come after him. As he slowly moved from that position, he could hear VC voices from deep in the jungle, and they sounded like they were in several locations. It wasn't much longer when he heard four shots from what he thought was Yate's rifle, taking out some of the enemies. The birds, insects, and everything suddenly went silent, and he realized the VC was looking for him and Yates. Now, instead of being the hunter, he was being hunted. He wasn't sure where the VC was, so he slowly returned to the LZ, hid in the tree line in the thick brush, and waited for Yates and the chopper.

Because of the number of the enemy in the area, Doug kept waiting at the LZ until it was time for the chopper pilot to pick them up. He waited quietly, hidden for a few hours, but it seemed forever. The chopper was right on time, and there was still no sign of Yates. Doug could hear the "thwap," "thwap," and "thwap" of the chopper blades as they approached the LZ. Just as the pilot was getting ready to sit it down, Yates ran to the chopper from across the other side of the open field.

The surrounding jungle erupted in hundreds of small arms fire from the VC hiding in the tree line. All Doug could do was watch in horror as Yates was hit several times by enemy gunfire and went down. Once the chopper started receiving incoming fire, and the pilot knew that Yates was dead, he didn't land; he immediately took off and was out of sight in just a matter of seconds. He thought, "The sound that I so loved a few minutes earlier, I'm now dreading to hear." He waited until all he could hear was the faint "thwap" off in the distance. He was left in the jungle, and it would be up to him to survive and find his way back to his camp.

The VC ran over to Yate's body and shot him several times to ensure he was dead. Doug knew he was in deep trouble, and the VC were all around him, so he had to get out of there, or he would soon die. He figured that soon, his artillery might be called in, and they would fire on the position and maybe even airstrikes since so many VCs were spotted in the area. Regardless, he knew he had to get out of there before he became a Vietnam casualty. He started very quietly to find his way deep into the jungle. He tried to figure out his position from the fading sun and knew it would be his camp's direction if he headed east.

He was right. The American Military had brought in gunships, artillery, and planes and bombed the area behind him. He became exhausted after creeping through the jungle for several hours until late in the night. He decided to find a place to rest and hide until daylight.

Doug didn't get any sleep that night; he was so cold and scared he felt like he could hear his teeth chattering. Even though Vietnam got hot and humid during the day, the nights were sometimes very chilly. While hiding and waiting for daylight, he had many thoughts going through his head. For the first time since he had been in Vietnam, he felt afraid for his own life. He wondered what the VC would do to him if they found him. Would they immediately kill him, torture him, and then kill him? He knew snipers were among the most feared and hated soldiers because they killed their enemies. Insects were making different noises, and he was praying a deadly Viper snake didn't crawl up next to him and strike him as he moved.

He sat in total silence, and he could hear his heartbeat pounding in his chest. He was hoping that as loud as it sounded to him, the VC couldn't hear it. He tried to collect his thoughts and plan his strategy as he sat alone in the thick jungle cover. When he looked up through the trees, there were millions of stars, and his thoughts were on Shirley and Jenifer and how much he missed them. He wondered if anyone except Shirley cared what he was going through.

The following day, just as the sun started rising, Doug headed east again. He wasn't sure where the VC was in relation to his position but believed they were somewhere close on his trail. He knew they were hunting him and would not give up until they found him. He had to make sure he covered his urine because he heard that the VC could smell the Americans while in the jungles. They could smell the soap used on their bodies, their cigarettes, and their discharged urine. He had a little water left from his canteen, but. He wanted to save some of it if he had to be in the jungle for a while. He put the canteen to his dry lips and took a few tiny swallows.

He made his way through the jungle and crept along until night. It was his second night alone, and he wondered if he would leave the jungle alive.

He had heard about American soldiers captured, tied upside down in trees, skinned alive, and then left to die. Of all the ways they could kill him, he felt that would be the most inhumane way for him to die. The one thing that kept him focused on trying to get out of the jungle alive was the thought of someday seeing Jenifer and Shirley again. It started to rain Late in the evening, and the torrential rains in Vietnam always stopped everything.

The rain had slowed down during the night, but Doug could fill his canteen with much-needed water. At dawn, he was up and slowly moving east. Several hours later, he came to a big open area about a quarter-mile from the tree line on the other side. It looked like it went for miles in both directions, so there was no way around it. It had grass about three feet high, but that was the only cover in the open field.

As he contemplated the options, he thought, "This could be it for me; if the VC is on my trail and waiting for me to pop out in the open, they will kill me for sure." If he wanted to continue east, he had no alternative but to start across the open field. As soon as he got into the weeds, he attached some dry weeds to his clothing and helmet so that he would blend in with the rest of the weeds, and it would be hard for the VC to spot him as long as he took it easy and slow.

Sixty yards into the field, Doug realized there was a little creek, and the closer he got to it, he was in water and mud about knee-deep. The leeches were starting to crawl up his boots and pants. The mosquitoes were like a swarm of bees when you steal their honey. They were all over him, biting his hands and face. The leeches were all over his clothes, and he fought to peel them off as he went along. Now, he was fighting the VC and off leeches and mosquitoes.

Doug decided to rest and wait about fifteen minutes to see how close the VC was behind him. He didn't have to wait long when he saw three VCs dressed in black uniforms appear on the other side where he had just come. He was angry that they were still on his trail and close to him. He hoped and prayed they had given up the hunt for him after two days. He waited for them to get about sixty yards into the mud of the open field and then sat in and killed the VC that was bringing up the rear. The other two ducked and tried to hide in the weeds. As they turned and started to run for the tree line cover, he took careful aim and killed another one. By then, the third one could make it to the cover of the trees and getaway.

Doug knew, there was no doubt, they were hunting him, and there would be more that would take the place of the two he had killed. Now, the killing had become personal to him, and it was kill or be killed. He waited a few more minutes to see if the one that escaped would reappear, but he didn't. He took off the camouflage and headed east.

The VC encounter made Doug pick up his pace as he made his way through the jungle. He went as far as possible in the dark and found another place to hide for the night. The fact that the one VC had escaped created a sense of fear in him he had never felt before. The jungle was home to the VC, and he was in their backyard. He tried to stay awake as much as he could that night, but it was hard as he caught himself dozing off a few times. He tried to think happy about going home and being Shirley and Jenifer.

When the sun finally rose, it was the fourth day of his nightmare, and Doug was ragged-looking and exhausted. It was hot and humid, his uniform was dirty and sweaty, and he could hardly stand his body odor as he walked through the jungle. He kept looking back to see if he could spot the VC following him. His feet were starting to bother him because the inside of his boots was wet from the sweat. All he had eaten were insects he caught along the way. He could feel his body weakening from a lack of solid food and constantly fighting through the jungle. Every step he took, he kept thinking, man, it would be great to get a shower and some real food.

It was mid-afternoon of that fourth day when he finally came to a dirt road about forty feet wide in the middle of the jungle. It appeared to be traveled regularly. He got down and thanked God that he was out of the jungle. He found a place to hide on the side of the road and rest for a few minutes to see if the VC was close behind him.

After waiting for a while and not seeing any VC, he headed toward his camp. After a few hours, he heard a vehicle coming in his direction, so he got off the road and hid in the woods. He could tell it was a United States Army truck when it got closer. When it was close, he walked into the center of the road with his weapon. He had it in the air as if to surrender.

The soldiers in the truck could see he was frail as he fell to his knees. The soldier on the passenger side had a rifle pointed at Doug as he got out of the truck and started asking him questions about what he was doing in the middle of the jungle. Doug explained that he was with a sniper unit and had been left in the jungle. The soldiers were familiar with his unit and had heard what had happened to him and Yates, so they gave him a ride back to his base camp.

Once Doug was in his headquarters, he ate and rested for a few days. They brought him before his commanding officer, and he told Doug they had given up hope of finding him alive and had reported him as missing in action (MIA). The commander stated, "Everyone figured there wasn't any way you could have gotten out alive, especially after the chopper pilot told us about Yates and the number of VCs in the area." It was also just as Doug had suspected; they had hit the entire area with airstrikes and artillery once they couldn't get the two of them out. It was good that he went into the jungle when he did, or he may have been killed by "friendly fire" (our military).

That was Doug's most frightening experience in Vietnam, but it made him realize an important life lesson: he had only himself. He discovered you can't always count on others to bail you out when things get tough. That's when he came up with his belief that the only place you can put your faith in is yourself and God.

After killing the North Vietnamese soldiers and the Viet Cong in South Vietnam for a year, his tour of duty was up, and the Army sent him back to the United States to serve the rest of his military time. After a leave of absence, he still had about five months left to go home and see Shirley and Jennifer. He was sent to Fort Benning, Georgia, to be a sniper instructor for his remaining months. Although he never liked his time in the military, he did his patriotic duty, and after two years, he was discharged from the Army's active duty status.

***

Chapter 4 - Life Changes

Once Doug returned to his hometown, he decided he wanted to do something with his life that was constructive. He tried to save lives instead of taking them. He thought he had done and seen enough killing and destruction in Vietnam to last him his lifetime.

Doug talked to Shirley about his plan to become a doctor and asked her if she would be willing to get a job and help while attending college and medical school. It would take several years of medical school and residency.

Once Doug was in school, Shirley got a job as a receptionist, and in a few years, she became a Dental Assistant. Along with Doug working various jobs, her income was enough to keep food on the table and pay the bills. She seemed to be happy with their arrangement and never complained.

Soon, Doug completed his residency at the local Hospital in Visalia. He felt great that he could finally remove some of Shirley's burdens. Jenifer was around ten years old then, and she was growing up way too fast by the time he set up his practice. He was so busy building his physician practice that he never had much family time unless he set aside specific dates during the year. He was not only spending nine or ten hours a day seeing patients but was called in the middle of the night for emergency patients.

In a few short years, Doug paid back all his student loans and purchased a house on a large lot in Green Acres Estates. It was an older but exclusive area of Visalia, and the lots were about a half-acre in size. There were many full-grown trees and plants, so they didn't feel like they were so close to the next-door neighbor. They had a twenty-foot driveway on the east side of the house and a twenty-foot by forty-foot metal building in the back.

Doug kept his small fishing boat inside and set up a home gym in the building to work out three to four days a week. They purchased a thirty-foot Four Winds motor home and parked it in front of the building. They envisioned someday traveling and enjoying sight-seeing throughout the United States when Doug retired, and Jenifer was out of school and independent.

Doug's brother Randy and his wife Karen lived in Visalia with their two children, sons and daughters.

Jenifer met David Hunter during her senior year in high school. David had just graduated from the local junior college and worked in the sales department at his family's lumberyard. He was a tall, slender young man with brown hair and green eyes. He always seemed to be in a good mood and happy. It was easy to see what Jenifer saw in him. His father had died from a sudden heart attack during his first year of college, so he had to help with the family business. He was making a good income, and only a year after her graduation did he and Jenifer decide to get married.

The day came, and their new grandson, Michael Douglas Hunter, was born. Doug took time off work and ensured he could be there when Michael was born. His entire world changed when his grandson came into the world. He decided to start taking more time off from work and spend more time with his family. After Michael was born, he would call Jenifer and talk to her a few times during the week, and he and Shirley would babysit Michael as often as they could to be with him. Doug loved watching Michael learn how to crawl, walk, and utter his first words: mommy, daddy, papa, and gamma.

The family was torn apart when Michael was only two and a half years old. David and Jenifer had left Michael with Doug and Shirley to attend a function they had to attend in the evening. It was around 1:00 a.m. when they received a call from the local police that there had been a terrible car accident involving a drunk driver, and Jennifer and David didn't make it.

After Jenifer's death, Doug and Shirley spent all their time with Michael, teaching him how to share, play with other kids, mind the teachers, and respect his elders. Michael wasn't deprived of anything, and yet he very seldom misbehaved. He was always happy and respectful to others. Doug took Michael with him everywhere he went, even if it was just to the store and back. He liked to brag about his grandson to all the people in the stores. He would tell everyone what a good kid he was.

Doug taught Michael to ride a bike, snow ski, water ski, and fish. They enrolled Michael in the youth football program when he was old enough, and they did everything with and for him. They also enrolled Michael in a private Christian school so he could get the best education available.

The next several years with Michael were spent watching him grow from a boy to a young man. He was almost six feet tall when he was sixteen years old. Doug and Shirley continued to devote their entire life to raising him and spent every spare moment they could with him. They continued to go to countless football games, play video games with him, or hang out together, sometimes just watching television. They laughed with each other as Michael went through the "awkward years" with the girls. They made it a daily point to tell each other how much they loved each other. As Michael grew older, Doug's bond with him was so strong that he felt he wasn't only his grandson and best friend. They could talk about anything, regardless of the subject. They never lost their temper or had harsh words to say to each other.

During Michael's second year of high school, Shirley came down with stage 4 breast cancer. She went through all the usual treatment of surgery and chemotherapy, but none of it worked. She died almost a year later when Michael was a Junior in high school. Doug and Michael were devastated by her loss. That's when Michael told Doug he would join the United States Army after graduating high school. At first, Doug tried to talk him out of it, but nothing he could say would change Michael's mind.

* * *

Chapter 5 - Michael's in the Army

Michael immediately signed up for military Special Force training when he graduated from high school. When Michael arrived at the Fort Benning Army Base, he was treated to the same familiar introductory basic training welcome he had seen in the movies when he was younger. He knew it wouldn't be easy, so he had prepared himself to handle anything the Army had in store for him. He was assigned immediately to the Infantry One Station Unit Training OSUT.

That's when Doug was truly alone, so he started studying and learning everything he could about Muslim Terrorist organizations. The more Doug learned about the radical terrorist organizations, the more complicated he thought they were to figure out. They weren't just one easy-to-defeat organization; there were many radical terrorist organizations. They had tons of money behind them, so they could purchase the best weapons to carry out their acts of terror. They had people in their heads, like Osama bin Laden, who had been planning and carrying out terrorist attacks worldwide for years.

According to what he read on the internet before September 11, 2001, Muslims heard shouting statements from local meetings saying things like, "Kill the Jews, and destroy the West." Books, pamphlets, and promotional materials were passed out at their conventions. Also, some of their mosques called for the "extermination of the Jews and Christians." When they were questioned about some of their activities and things they were saying in their mosques and other gathering places in America, they just said, "It is our civil right to say what we want in America." (17)

Doug read material from American Journalist Steven Emerson, the founder and Executive Director of the Investigative Project on Terrorism for the United States. He and his staff have provided briefings to the United States Government and law enforcement agencies, members of Congress, and Congressional Committees regarding terrorist organizations. (17)

Reading tons of other material on the available internet gave Doug considerable insight into the hearts and minds of radical terrorist groups. He became even more determined to learn their language and everything he could about them. He figured by the time Michael was through with all his training. He would have a real good idea of where the radical Muslim terrorist organizations in America were.

Doug decided to buy a sniper rifle during Michael's long training phase and do some target shooting. The legal target shooting area is near Barstow, California. Doug wondered if he could still hit a target from a long distance.

Doug found out where the next big gun show would be held near his area. He found out that one was coming up in Reno, Nevada, so he decided to take a six-hour drive and check it out. When he got to the show, he looked at many different weapons. After watching and talking to several gun dealers throughout the day, he finally found the one he wanted.

The gun dealer asked him what kind of weapon he was talking about, and Doug explained the type, model, and everything he wanted. He looked at Doug with one eye shut, and the wrinkles in his face deepened as he said, "A gun like that will cost you a lot of money with everything you want on it, plus the ammunition." He told the gun dealer he would give him the cash to get the rifle and five hundred rounds of ammunition. Doug also asked for a pistol with a silencer and one hundred rounds of ammo for it as well. He agreed to give him half the money and half when he got the two weapons.

Doug was about to give up on the gun dealer after a month passed when he got a call. It was the gun dealer, and he told him he had the rifle, the pistol, and all the accessories he wanted. Doug made the drive to Utah and picked them up.

Once back, he made four wooden targets out of one-inch plywood that were the size of a person from the waist up. He painted two of them black and two dark green. The following day, he loaded his rifle, pistol, and ammunition and headed for the desert. It was about a three-hour and forty-five-minute drive from Visalia to the spot Doug had picked to shoot his weapons. He packed lunch in a small ice chest.

Once at his destination, he set his targets at approximately two hundred yards, three hundred yards, and five hundred yards from his firing position. Although his hearing wasn't as good as it used to be, his eyesight was still excellent. He scoped in on his two-hundred-yard target, quietly let out his breath, and slowly squeezed the trigger. It took him several shots to get used to the rifle, but he loved how it felt. He hit all three other targets within seven or eight inches of where he was aiming.

As soon as Michael received the news that he had made it through the ninety-five-week training program and would be graduating, he called Doug and told him the graduation would be in a few weeks, and he wanted him to come. Doug was excited to hear from Michael and learn he had made it through all Special Forces Course phases. After he had hung up the phone, Doug immediately made arrangements with the airline and hotel.

When he arrived at the airport, Michael greeted Doug with a giant bear hug. They both had big smiles and tears as they looked at each other.

Doug stared at him and said, "Man, I missed you."

As emotion caught in his throat, Michael could hardly speak, "I missed you too, grandpa."

Doug couldn't believe how much more mature Michael looked. Unlike the young guy he last remembered, he looked like a grown man. His mind flashed back to the little boy that he had watched grow. All those years flashed before Doug's eyes in a split second. He thought, Oh my God, where had all the time gone?

Doug went to the ceremony the next day, and afterward, Michael came over to Doug and asked, "How did you like the ceremony, Grandpa?"

Doug told him he enjoyed it and how proud he was. While talking with each other, Michael was holding some papers that looked important in his hands.

Doug looked down at them and said, "Orders?"

Michael held them up and said, "I received them a few minutes ago. They're the orders for my next duty station. I get a 30-day leave of absence, and then I'm being deployed to Afghanistan with my 12-man A-Team."

On his way home, Doug was sad and apprehensive about Michael going to Afghanistan.

On Thursday, January 12, 2009, Michael called Doug and told him he would be at the Fresno Airport around 4:00 p.m. Michael was dressed in his Army Green uniform when he stepped off the plane. They were both excited to see each other.

When he opened the trunk of his Mercedes, the target shooting boards were still there, and Michael said, "Hey, Grandpa, what's this?"

Doug grinned and proudly said, "I purchased a British sniper rifle with a scope and everything. I've been target shooting out in the desert."

The excitement and adrenaline of being home finally caught up with him. "I have your room ready for you, just like you left it."

As he headed for the bedroom, he replied, "Thanks, Grandpa. I'll see you a little later."

Doug grinned and said, "Get some sleep, and I'll see you in the morning."

The following day, Doug had already been up a few hours by the time Michael walked into the kitchen with his messy, short hair. He had made his favorite breakfast: fluffy pancakes smothered in butter, three "over easy" fried eggs, and a half-pound of extra crispy bacon.

Michael's eyes widened, "I can't wait to dig in. Thanks for breakfast, Grandpa."

Doug laughed, "Don't get too used to it. I won't do it daily, or you'll be waddling to your next duty station."

They both laughed as Michael reached for the syrup.

While at breakfast, Michael asked him how his car was running.

Doug said, "I drove it a few times a month down to the local Stop and Go Market just to ensure it would be ready for you when you got home."

Michael's eyes widened with happiness as he said, "How would you feel about us going for a little drive after I shower?"

Doug said, "That would be great. I'll shower and meet you in the garage."

After driving around town for a few hours, Michael finally saw everything he wanted, and they headed back home.

When they arrived home, Michael went to the outside building and saw that Doug had made the room into a bit of a workshop, but the weights, stationary bike, and treadmill were still there. The covered fishing boat was at the other end of the building.

Michael rubbed the hull, saying, "It's too bad it's winter. We could've taken the boat out for the day. I'd love to hook into a couple of those big trout." He was still unsure what to do with the rest of the days he had left before he was deployed to Afghanistan, but knew he would spend as much time with his grandpa as possible.

Michael hadn't shaved since he came home on leave. He was told that growing facial hair and wearing local clothing is one way the Green Berets blend in among the locals along the Pakistan border in Afghanistan. He told Doug that the Green Berets in Afghanistan are called the "Bearded Bastards" by the insurgents that prowl the steep mountains and narrow valleys of the remote area near Chamkani, Afghanistan. It's supposed to be where conventional forces usually can't go. He told Doug his team would train locals to fight against the Taliban, al-Qaeda, and other insurgents in Afghanistan.

Even though Doug had his opinion of the war, its people, and American politics, he didn't want to tell Michael that he was more than just scared for his safety. He was terrified of him going to Afghanistan. He couldn't bear the thought of his grandson being killed by a Muslim terrorist organization in Afghanistan. At the same time, he wouldn't discourage Michael by telling him how he felt about his deployment.

The next day, Michael had everything packed and ready to go. Doug was sad to see him leave but didn't tell him how unhappy he was. He drove him to the airport and waited with him until he boarded the plane. The last thing they said to each other in person as they hugged was, "I love you." As the plane flew off, Doug watched it until it was out of sight, and again, he had that familiar sick feeling in the pit of his stomach. This time, it was different; he watched his grandson head to Afghanistan's hostile lands thousands of miles from home. He wasn't sure if he would ever see Michael alive again.

* * *

Afghanistan is a landlocked country in South West Asia. Michael had no idea where he was going in Afghanistan until he arrived because all Special Forces soldiers' activities are classified and top secret. He knew he would fly into the Kandahar International Airport in Afghanistan. He had met up with the rest of his team before they left the States. They were all together on the flight to Afghanistan.

The Kandahar Airport is the primary airport used by the United States Special Forces in Afghanistan. NATO armies also use this airport for shipping and receiving supplies. The other major airport is in Kabul, the capital of Afghanistan. Sometimes, sandstorms can affect air travel in Afghanistan, not allowing flights in or out. (1)

When Michael and his team arrived in February, the temperature was about thirty-two degrees. It had just snowed a few days earlier, and the snow was still on the ground. He didn't think the weather would be a problem, except for the snow, because it was like his hometown. One thing he knew for sure was that it was cold when he stepped off the plane in Kandahar.

Michael was ordered to head to Kunduz, near the Hindu Kush Mountains in northeastern Afghanistan. He was put on a Chinook helicopter, and the rest of his "A" team went to their new home. Now that he was with his team, he no longer focused on himself. He was concerned about the rest of his team members and what they could do to survive this tour of duty.

Over the past two years, before Michael arrived, Kunduz and Baghlan's Northern provinces' security had deteriorated. The Taliban and allied terror groups also maintain safe havens in Baghlan and Kunduz and control large portions of the provinces of the seven districts in the Kunduz province. The Taliban was beginning to step up their attacks in the area. It was one of the main reasons Michael had been deployed to this area with his Special Forces Team. According to reports, the Taliban commander for Kunduz province vowed in 2008 to increase his men's efforts against the United States and the Allied forces. The Taliban mainly relied upon suicide bombings and I.F.D.s (improvised explosive devices).

During Michael's time at Kunduz, he kept in touch with Doug and let him know how he was doing. That gave Doug some sense of security regarding his safety since he didn't always know what Michael's daily activities involved. He was always relieved to hear from Michael and told him he loved him. Michael would always say, "I love you too, Grandpa," each time before he hung up the phone.

In May 2009, Michael's team was deployed by helicopters into a Taliban hideout in Ghor Tapa, about seven miles northwest of Kunduz. Upon landing, fierce fighting broke out, and one of Michael's close team members was hit in the shoulder by an enemy small arms fire. Michael quickly pulled him aside and started to administer medical aid. He gave him some morphine to ease the pain until they could get him medevac. After attending to him, Michael grabbed his rifle and joined in the assault. During the ensuing battle, several militants and three Taliban commanders were killed. Several insurgents were captured. The entire firefight lasted several minutes, and then it was over. Michael attended to his teammate while he was medevac back to the military base hospital.

Once the mission was over and Michael was back at the safe house, he called Doug and told him about the five-day mission and how the Allied forces had killed several of the Taliban and captured others. Doug asked him if he was in the firefight. Michael knew how he felt about being in the middle of the fighting, so he reluctantly said, "At times, I was firing my weapon, but I spent most of my time taking care of wounded soldiers."

Doug could feel the fear of losing Michael creep up from the pit of his stomach to his throat as he told him.

"Don't try to be a hero. You're all I've left, and I don't want to lose you."

Michael tried his best to assure him he would be okay, "Don't worry, Grandpa, I promise I won't. I'm not doing anything stupid, and always try to avoid fighting. I love you, and I will talk to you again soon."

Little did they know that would be the last conversation they would ever have with each other.

The Army officials reported that Michael was killed on December 2, 2009, along with two other Special Forces soldiers from his Team. A terrorist I.E.D. killed them.

When the Army soldiers arrived at Doug's door, he was shocked as they gave him the news of Michael's death. At first, he didn't believe them. He told them they must have made a mistake because Michael was a medical sergeant and didn't see that much combat. He was having a hard time believing that it had happened. He thought this might have been a mistaken identity case, or perhaps Michael was just wounded and lying in a military hospital somewhere. He asked them if they were positive it was Michael, and they said there was no question that it was him. They pulled out his dog tags and gave them to him. Trying to control his emotions, he asked them when they would send his body home.

After the soldiers left, Doug shut the door, dropped to his knees, and started weeping. Deep down in his soul, the cries of his pain were as he yelled out, "You terrorist will pay for Michael's death. I promise you I will hunt you down and destroy you." For the first time in his life, he knew what genuine hatred was because he felt for the terrorists. There was nothing he could do to control his anger and pain. At that moment, it felt like someone had sucker-punched him in the chest and ripped out his heart while it was still beating. He hit the door to the bathroom with his fist as he went in to get napkins to wipe away the tears.

Over the next few hours, he kicked furniture, hit walls, and slammed the refrigerator with his open palms. At one point, he gripped the kitchen table with all his strength and tried to squeeze away the pain. Nothing seemed to help because the finality of Michael's death was almost more than he could bear. The one thing he feared the most for Michael had come true. Now that Michael had died at the hands of these radical Muslim terrorists, Doug would not let his death go unpunished. He told himself that he would inflict the most profound pain on them and their organizations. More than anything, he wanted them to feel his pain at that moment.

It was several hours before Doug called his brother and told him the news. He was awake all night as thoughts of Michael ran through his mind. He kept wondering if there was something more he could've done to persuade Michael to stay out of the military. He tossed and turned as he beat himself up all night.

The next day, Michael's friends found out about his death and called to give their condolences. Doug didn't remember much about who called. Most days leading up to and after Michael's funeral were a blur. He went through all the motions but just felt numb inside. He felt like he was in some bad dream and would wake up and find out Michael was still alive. Regardless of his hard work, he couldn't wake up from the bad dream.

It was during the funeral that the reality of Michael's death finally hit him the hardest. That's when he came to grips with the fact that radical Muslim terrorists had killed Michael. He received the full military funeral, and they gave Doug the customary folded-up American Flag.

When the military officials handed it to him, all he could think of at the time was, after everything they had been through together. The notice is all he has left of Michael except the memories. The hatred and need for revenge toward the terrorists were eating at him and holding him together.

For several days after Michael's funeral, Doug was in a daze as he walked around the house and in and out of Michael's room. Even though he was sad, angry, and empty inside, he talked to Michael and told him his next move against the cowardly terrorist organizations.

* * *

Chapter 7 - Doug Plots His Revenge

After Michael's funeral, all Doug could think about was the radical terrorist insurgents that had killed him. He started planning his strategy to get even with them for killing Michael. While racking his brain, he thought about how angry he was with the politicians because the two wars had gone on for so long, and American soldiers were still fighting and dying in the Foreign land.

He couldn't help himself; the more he thought about Michael's death, the more he developed his deep-seated hatred for all the radical Muslim terrorist organizations. After days of planning and contemplating, he decided to declare war on all the radical Muslim terrorist organizations hiding in America.

He knew he couldn't do anything about them in their own countries, but he could do something about them in America. He wouldn't wait for any more attacks without doing his part to try to stop them. He would hurt the terrorist where they would feel it the most, in their gathering places, mosques, compounds, and training camps, right here in America.

He was going to find out how to make and use the same bombs the terrorists had used to kill Michael. He was also going to kill as many of them as possible with his sniper rifle and pistol.

A few days later, he had tears running down his cheeks as he shouted aloud, "I'll kill them at their own terrorist game, Michael. I'll hunt them down until I find their little hiding places and destroy them. When I find them, I'll blow them to pieces!" He was like a man who had become obsessed as the days went by and became focused on his plan. He'd now become consumed with his plan.

Doug decided his motor home would become his new home while he carried out his attacks. He went to the shop and had a car hitch on his motor home to tow his Mercedes. He went to the local camera store and purchased a Nikon camera. The camera would be one of his decoys, and he would keep it in the front seat and on the passenger side when he was traveling from target to target. Law enforcement would tell them he was a senior tourist citizen, just taking pictures if stopped. He wanted to appear as an older retired man traveling around in his motor home, taking photos of the scenery, and seeing America's sites.

He mapped out the areas where the terrorist cells were suspected in America. He planned to find a campground within a fifty-mile radius of his targets and set up camp for a few days with his motor home. He would then unhitch his car, drive it to his targets, place his bombs, and blow them up. After he started his bombings, he would move from location to location, where it would be hard for law enforcement to pinpoint him.

His next project was to spend a few days redoing the back seat of his Mercedes. He cut out the rear seat springs where he would have a place to hide his sniper rifle. Once he had the springs out, he built a wooden box compartment for the rifle and I.E.D. s so a few would fit under the seat. When he was done with the box, he ensured the seat fit back in place and looked normal, even with everything inside. He ensured that it wasn't easily detectable by someone just looking in the windows.

He purchased a professional metal detector as another decoy and placed it in the trunk, along with an entrenching shovel. If he got pulled over by law enforcement and looked in his trunk, they would think it was to dig up hidden treasures. Over the shoulder carrying bag, the metal detectors black was also the perfect size to carry Doug's rifle, scope, and a few I.E.D.

He went to the Army Surplus store, purchased several six-inch foam layer mats, and lined the compartment underneath his motor home, where he would store additional I.E.D. s. He bought two sets of camouflage uniforms that would fit over his clothing and one camouflaged Gilly suit.

Doug had a friend who owned a Pest Control business, so he talked him into giving him a couple of uniforms with his logo. He had the phone numbers on the shirts changed to fake cell phone numbers. He went to Orchard Supply and purchased a sprayer that looked like a commercial unit he could carry on his back. While there, he also purchased a pesticide in the sprayer, just in case he had to use it. He believed this would help him get close to a few of his targets as a pest control agent.

After extensive internet research, he soon learned how to make and explode the I.E.D.'s bombs like the ones that had killed Michael in Afghanistan. He drove to Los Angeles and spent two days locating a (fence), a guy he felt he could trust to purchase all the material he needed to make the bombs. He knew he could buy whatever he needed if he had enough money, so he brought plenty of cash so that money wouldn't be his problem. While there, he had his contact get 60 blocks of C-4 plastic explosives with detonators and a remote-control detonator. Each block was one and a quarter pounds. He also had him get one hundred pounds of steel balls the size of marbles. It took four days for his contact to get what he had on his list, but he could come up with everything Doug wanted.

While waiting for his contact to return, he had a fake I.E.D. printed with Douglas Youssef's name. It was the name he would use when he needed to show a phony identity. He knew the type of clothing the Muslim people typically wore during their meetings. While in Los Angeles, he went to several stores and purchased the ceremonial robes and black Middle Eastern attire he needed. He also purchased two dark, long-haired wigs with graying streaks and two graybeards with mustaches attached. He ensured he bought the materials so they would stick to his face and head without coming loose. He wanted to make sure he fitted in with the Muslim population when he went into their mosques or other compounds to spy on them.

He also purchased a black hooded sweatshirt and black wool ski cap to pull down over his ears.

When he got back to Visalia, he feverishly started his task of making the bombs in his workshop. He was a man that was obsessed, and nothing was going to stand in his way. He had several boxes of disposable gloves from his medical practice, and when he made the bombs, he used the gloves to ensure there were no fingerprints on anything. He spent tedious hours making the bombs all day, and for everyone he made, he took satisfaction in knowing he was getting closer to starting his mission.

He wanted to make at least twenty I.E.D. s before he went on his first hunt to find his targets. Each I.E.D. had a pound of C-4 and about four hundred steel balls packed in each. It would be like firing four hundred rounds from a rifle during the explosion when the bomb blew up. It was enough to destroy a vehicle and several people within the area of the bomb.

One afternoon, while he was making one of the I.E.D. s, Michael's best friend Gary came by to say hello. Because Doug was working in his shop and had the music playing loud, he didn't hear Gary knock on the door. He could see Doug working but wasn't getting a response, so he opened the door and went in. When Doug heard the door close behind him, he was startled that Gary was already inside the building. He turned his head and shoulder toward Gary to say hello and quickly threw a towel over the bomb material he was working on so Gary couldn't see it.

When Doug turned toward him, he said, "Hey, Doctor Cotton, I knocked on the door, but you didn't hear me. I hope you don't mind. I just came by to see how you're doing." Doug quickly turned the music down, walked toward him, put his arm around his shoulders, and headed for the exit.

Gary asked, "So what are you working on?" Doug said, "Oh, I'm just tinkering around to try and keep myself busy."

He said, "Let's go inside, have a soda, and visit."

Gary was hoping for that because he wanted to talk about Michael.

After Gary left, Doug mentally kicked himself because that was too close for comfort. He was almost caught right in the middle of making one of the bombs, and that would've been a total disaster. From then on, he would ensure the shop door was locked when working inside. He didn't want anyone to discover what he was working on and ruin his plans.

Doug spent his nights reading everything he could about his future targets. He wanted to know where they were in America. It was hard to pinpoint their exact locations, but he found some information that gave him the city and states. Even though he had all that information, he would still have to go and hunt them down. To search for any information he could find on terrorist organizations.

The September 11, 2001 hijackers were operating as sleeper cells before they acted that day. They traveled to Las Vegas and participated in gambling and other activities without paying attention to their actual goals. Effective terrorist cells are usually tiny and tightly managed, generally three to four people, rarely involving more than ten or twenty. The September 11, 2011 operation was conducted by four sleeper cells composed of about three to five individuals per cell. Because of their nature, these groups are tough to track down and easy for them to infiltrate due to their small size.

Illegal immigrants can live outside the government's scope of detection. One of the main reasons is that America has a 4,000-mile border to the North with Canada and over 2,000 miles to the South with Mexico. Slipping in and out of our borders has always been very easy. Thousands of people illegally cross the borders daily through tunnels dug, smuggled, or other ways. (16) No one knows what weapons of mass destruction they bring with them.

There have been reports that Middle Eastern and Asian people paying for safe passage through the border holes have grown since September 11, 2001. According to government estimates, as many as twelve million illegal aliens live in the United States.

The more Doug read about the different terrorist organizations that supported Jihad in America and worldwide, the more he realized that the United States has just been fighting the beginning of its fight against terror in the world. He believed that the home-grown terrorist organizations in the United States weren't going to do anything but grow in numbers.

In his mind, Doug believed he had to do something about them because all the terrorist organizations were guilty of killing his grandson. It was his country, the place he loved, and he wasn't going to let a radical Muslim-born American or some other radical foreign terrorist organization destroy or kill any more Americans. He knew he couldn't stop them all, but at least he believed he could slow them down and make the government and the American people more aware they were here in America preaching their hatred. He felt that maybe if he could bring attention to them, the American people would rise and protest their existence and possibly expel them from America.

What was astonishing to Doug is that the freedoms that allow the radical Muslim terrorist organization to exist in America are precisely what the terrorists despise most about the United States (They hate the western way of life). Doug believed that many Americans have not come to grips with or are not aware of the amount and desire of their genuine threat to us as a nation. Doug wondered if we would sit with our heads buried in the sand and let them commit another September 11, 2001, or if we would stop them before it was too late.

Doug had seen in Vietnam how the communist Viet Cong and North Vietnamese soldiers would kill their people if they believed they could kill a few American soldiers. They had no regard for human life if it meant accomplishing their goal of destroying their enemy. He believed the radical Islamic terrorist organizations operate the same way. He was stunned and angry when he learned that the radical Islamic Terrorist Organizations were using America as one of the major countries to plan and train to spread terror throughout the world.

* * *

Chapter 8 - Doug's First Target

He was startled to find a suspected terrorist training camp in his backyard just southeast of Fresno and northeast of Visalia in a remote area of the foothills during his research. The camp contained eighteen hundred acres and was once owned and occupied by a drug addict recovery cult. The compound has mobile homes, a huge cafeteria, buildings, and a large airplane landing strip. According to all the information he had found, it was now occupied by a Muslim terrorist organization.

He read in the local newspaper to confirm Doug's suspicions of the compound. He had seen on the news that a Fresno County Sherriff was killed at the suspected terrorist camp by a twenty-year-old Muslim while the Sherriff was trying to apprehend him for a simple burglary charge. (1)

The reports he read said it was suspected of being used by a Muslim terrorist organization to train their people in hand-to-hand combat, rifles, explosives, and grenades.

Foothill neighbors of the camp had reported hearing excessive gunfire and explosions from the compound since the Muslims took over the compound a few years earlier. The neighbors said it sounded like military training was happening in the compound. Doug knew it would be easy to hide that activity because of the camp's size. As he read the information, he thought this training camp would be easy to sneak into and plant one of his bombs or maybe two if they don't have guards on duty twenty-four hours a day. Even though it was fenced with private gates along the main roads and the compound's perimeter, he would hide and observe it for a few days. He would find out where they hid their weapons and did training.

The camp was about an hour's drive from Visalia on a slow, winding, narrow road. Even though it was slow traveling to get there, it had easy access from the road, and hiding his car in the trees away from the main camp entrance would be easy. Doug got up around 4:00 a.m. one morning, put on his camouflage clothing, made his way to the camp, and set up his observation point before daylight. As he watched, he saw a lot of activities in the camp.

On the third day of observing them, he noticed a group of men that marched in what looked like a military march, with a person directing them to one of the buildings. It was located away from the cafeteria and the main buildings. Once there, all the men took turns going into the building and coming out with AK-47 weapons strapped across their shoulders. Once they had their weapons, they marched to a secluded area, and Doug observed them as they did target practice. He also watched them throwing grenades and other explosives. He knew they were doing some military training. That went on for a couple of hours, and then the men marched back to the building and put the rifles away. They then marched to an area where they received instructions in hand-to-hand combat. This training continued for a few more hours there. He didn't notice any armed guards along the perimeter, so he assumed they might feel safe in this location.

The building where they stored all their weapons was his target. He figured if he blew it up, the very least that would happen would bring law enforcement to the camp to investigate what was happening there.

Before doing anything, he wanted to take a little of the C-4 and a couple of I.E.D. s to the desert, use the remote-control detonator, and ensure everything worked correctly. He spent a day in the desert testing the bombs, and after using a small amount of the C-4 and blowing up one of the I.E.D. s, he was convinced he wouldn't have any problem carrying out his mission.

He waited a few days and ensured he had everything planned, including his escape route. Randy had a cabin up the road and past the little town of Dunlap. Doug believed that if he were pulled over by law enforcement, he could say he was heading up to his brothers' cabin or coming back from the house, depending on his direction when they stopped him.

Doug was very nervous the night of his first attack, pacing back and forth and going over everything in his mind. As he got ready to leave, he put two halves of the blocks of C-4, along with the detonators and the remote control, in the metal detector bag under the back seat of his car.

He made sure that all his clothing was black, including his shoes. He headed up to his target around midnight. When he got to the camp, he parked his car and took out the bag with his bombs. He ensured everything was there, threw it over his back, and stepped into the darkness.

Thank goodness he had been on the property when it was daylight because when he got there, it was so dark that he had to use the night vision goggles to see where he was going. He breathed heavily from excitement and fear as he reached his target. Once out of the tree line, he ducked down and stopped to take a few deep breaths. After watching everything for a few minutes, he crawled low on his belly and elbows and the remaining two hundred yards to the building.

When he arrived at the target building, he was shaking with anticipation as he attached one of the C-4 bombs and detonator to one side of the building. He went to another building, attached another C-4 bomb, and put in the detonator. He crawled back to the tree line, which was safe and hidden from view. He pushed the button and watched as the buildings each blew into pieces. There were several substantial secondary explosions from the explosives the terrorists had hidden in the buildings.

He quickly made his way back to his car. Once there, he put the empty bag and remote-control detonator under his seat and headed back down the winding roads toward Visalia.

On his way home, he was motioned to stop by a guy coming in the opposite direction. He was wearing a cowboy hat and driving a pick-up truck.

When Doug rolled down his window, he asked, "Did you see or hear any loud explosions up the road?"

Doug acted ignorantly and told him he was returning from a cabin up in the hills and didn't see or hear anything. He smiled at the cowboy and said, "I can't hear much when I have my Vince Gill CD cranked up loud."

The cowboy shrugged and said, "That's strange; it was pretty loud. It woke me up from my sleep."

Not getting the response he wanted from Doug, the cowboy thanked him and quickly headed further up the road in the camp's direction. Doug later thought about it, and a chill came over him. He didn't have any disguise, so he could've been easily identified if the cowboy had reported seeing him on that lonely dark road that night. Doug realized this was a huge mistake, no matter how much planning he had done. He knew that he would always have to wear a disguise during his attacks from that point on.

He didn't kill any terrorists on his first attack, but he had the satisfaction of knowing that it did bring law enforcement from Fresno and Tulare Counties up to the camp. The FBI was called to check things out because of the weapons found after the explosion. Doug knew the Muslim terrorists would have some heavy explaining to do about the weapons they had stashed in the building he blew up.

His first attack was a test; at the very least, he got the news media and law enforcement's attention. He also discovered that he could blow something up, giving him the confidence he needed to continue his mission. Even if they didn't shut down the camp, he figured it would put the Muslim terrorist training camp on high alert with law enforcement. He also knew it would be a while before they could acquire and hide more weapons at that location.

The next day, he watched on television as the local news reported the explosions and portrayed the camp people as peaceful, loving Muslims living in their little community in the foothills. The people near Fresno and Visalia were shocked and outraged to find out they had a suspected Muslim terrorist origination in the foothills and their back yards. Most people were like Doug and didn't realize this place existed before he blew up the buildings. As he watched the news reports, he was disgusted that if the Muslim people of this camp were such peaceful, loving people as they were claiming to be, why did they have a weapons cache, and why were they training?

Doug invited Randy and Karen to dinner at the Vintage Press Restaurant. During dinner, he told them he was cashing in some of his stocks and other investments, taking the motor home, and traveling around the United States, just like he and Shirley had always planned. He told them he would leave within the next few months and be gone before seeing them again. He told them he had deeded his house to them, and they could have it and all the furniture once he left. Randy and Karen were still in a little bit of shock as they left the restaurant. Once outside the restaurant, Doug assured them he would be financially comfortable for the rest of his life. Randy shook Doug's hand, Karen hugged him, and they all agreed to talk again soon.

* * *

Chapter 9 - Seattle and Portland

The day before Doug left for his next target in Seattle, he reviewed his checklist to ensure he had everything he needed. After reviewing his list several times, he hitched up his Mercedes to the motor home, went to the local gas station, and filled up all the tanks. He packed enough clothes in the motor home to last a few weeks. He had it parked in front of his house and ready to go early the following day.

That evening, he called Randy and told him he would be gone for a few weeks and that he wasn't taking any cell phones with him, so there wouldn't be any way to get in touch. He asked Randy to keep an eye on the place and ensure it didn't burn down.

Doug was up around 4:00 a.m. the following day, anxious and ready to get going. He had already showered and shaved and could hardly wait for the sixteen-hour drive to Seattle. It was a nine hundred and sixty-four-mile trip, so he thought he would stop somewhere around Medford, Oregon, at one of the rest stops and get a few hours of sleep before driving to Seattle.

Before he left, he took Michael's dog tags and put them around his neck. He looked in the mirror and could hardly recognize the person he had become. "Our new mission starts today, Michael, and I promise you, I will kill the terrorists for what they have done to you."

The place where he was headed was the campground at Washington State Park. It's along the saltwater shoreline on Puget Sound and has one of the most scenic views and wildlife watching in the United States. The park has three hiking trails, and Doug knew he would be using one of them. The campground was located halfway between the cities of Tacoma and Seattle. He thought this would be a perfect spot to set up his camp. The park had all the amenities that he needed to stay for several days if he had to.

Once there, he had to purchase a parking pass for his motor home and his car and made sure he paid for everything with cash. He thought having a café and espresso stand in the park was lovely. He wouldn't have to go far to have breakfast and lunches daily.

After getting everything situated with his motor home and relaxing for a few hours, he decided to take his Mercedes and go into Seattle to check things out. He had read articles about a Muslim training camp in Seattle. It was visited by a former Seattle resident who was sentenced to two years in federal prison in return for cooperating with federal investigators. He graduated from a local High School and was a Seattle entrepreneur who converted to Islam. He became an associate of a militant London cleric who was one of the people who praised the September 11, 2001, terrorist attacks. It was just the type of place Doug was after. (11)

Doug thought he would investigate around town and ask people a few questions about the Muslim activity in the area. He went to a secluded place, put on his Muslim disguise, and headed downtown, hoping to run into a few Muslims he could talk to regarding meetings or training activities. The guise was a perfect cover because he didn't want law enforcement to know that a clean-cut doctor asked around town about the Muslim organization just before one of their facilities was blown up.

After a few hours of asking questions at different locations, he was able to find out exactly what he needed to know. He found that a few homeless guys were his best source of information. They were more than willing to talk about anything they knew about the Muslim organization if he slipped them a few bucks. He found out it was common knowledge from the people in town that there used to be a Muslim terrorist training camp located about twenty miles out of town in a very secluded and wooded area. A couple of the guys he talked to said they heard the Muslims do target practice at the camp. They also thought the Feds had shut down the place a few years ago.

He got the general direction from one of the guys and decided to drive to where they thought the camp was in the woods. There was a locked gate when Doug arrived at the location, and no one was around. He looked over the area to see where people would park their cars inside the camp and where they did their shooting. The area had weeds over most of the camp and looked abandoned. He was disappointed that this would not be a good target for him.

After surveying the area, he drove back into Seattle to locate a mosque he had researched and would target. There were a couple of Muslim mosques not too far from the central part of downtown Seattle. One of them was the one he had read about that had suspected ties to several Muslim terrorist organizations. When he got to the mosque, people were dressed in traditional Middle Eastern attire. After everything he had read, there weren't a lot of so-called innocent by-standers in this suspected terrorist mosque. If these people allowed materials to be distributed from their mosque that said, "destroy Israel or Americans," he knew they were his targets.

It was a typical building sitting between two other commercial buildings and separated by about ten feet of space on each side. It had a little area resembling a front porch about eight feet wide by twelve long. Once Doug was satisfied this was the mosque, he drove back to the campground and got some much-needed sleep.

The next day Doug wanted to spend the entire day doing a little more poking around to see if he could find out more about the mosque without bringing a lot of attention. He wore his Muslim disguise and parked his car about four blocks from the mosque without being too conspicuous. After several hours of mingling with the people and listening to their hatred of the Jews and Christians, he was sure about blowing it up. Once back in his car, he removed his disguise, put it under the back seat, and returned to the campground. He waited until it was dark and loaded his C-4 bomb, along with his remote-control detonator, into his hiding place under the back seat of his car.

He had time to waste until midnight, so he decided to go to the Space Needle and have dinner. The restaurant rotates in 360-degree turns as you are eating. He loved the view of the City from there with all the lights and thought it was breathtaking. He wished he had Shirley, Jenifer, and Michael to share it. After dinner, it was time to head for the mosque to see what was going on, and it looked like everyone had left the building by the time he arrived.

He drove to the spot he had picked out earlier to park his car and waited until around 1:00 am. He put on his black sweatshirt and the black ski hat, took one block of the C-4, a detonator, and the small entrenching shovel and, put them in the black metal detector bag, then carried them to his target.

His heart was beating fast as he came up from the back of the building and crept slowly between the two buildings, hoping not to be seen. He planned to plant the bomb next to the porch. He dug a tiny area behind a plant, put in the block of C-4 and detonator, and lightly covered it. The ordeal took less than thirty seconds, and that part of his mission was over. He returned to the campground and tried his best to get some sleep but was having a hard time. He tossed and turned most of the night while thinking about his targets and Michael. He could finally go to sleep in the late hours of the morning.

When Doug got up the following day, he took his camera, walked around the campground, and took pictures of the ocean and wildlife. He was so nervous that he could hardly eat anything the entire day from the anticipation of his upcoming attack. It was like everything was in slow motion most of the day.

When evening came, he strapped the detonator to his chest and headed back to Seattle. He drove past the mosque, and men were talking outside the building. He went to where he had planned to park his car and then began walking toward the mosque. As he got within striking distance, he hit the detonator button, and, in a few seconds, the entire front of the mosque exploded in a thunderous explosion. At first, he was shocked at the blast's size as he went down in a ducking motion. He heard people screaming and running for cover. When he looked back, he saw flames and debris flying. He was thinking, take that, you terrorist scumbags. I hope I killed a lot of you.

He quickly turned and walked in the direction of his car. When he got there, he took off the remote detonator and put it under his back seat, got in the driver's seat, and just sat there for a minute and let out a massive sigh of relief. As he sat there in silence, he said, "This was the first one, Michael, but there will be many more. There is no turning back now." Even though he didn't feel like he was a terrorist like the people he was pursuing, he had become one of them by killing people with his bombs. He was now "The American Terrorist."

He drove back to his motor home, and by the time he got there, he was mentally drained from the emotion of bombing the mosque. Even though he didn't know the extent of the damage he'd caused, he was sure it was tremendous from the size of the explosion.

The next day, everyone in the campground talked about the mosque explosion, and he asked his neighbor in the camp next to him what had happened. The neighbor excitedly said, "According to the news reports, someone or some group blew up the local Muslim mosque and killed sixteen people and wounded about twelve others." Without showing emotion, Doug shook his head and said to himself. It's a shame I didn't get more of them. Deep down inside, he was delighted with himself for carrying out his mission successfully without any glitches or getting caught. He spent the rest of the day re-hooking his car to the motor home and getting ready to head to Portland.

Doug's next target was one hundred and seventy-four miles away and a three-hour drive south to Portland. He would stay at the Jantzen Beach RV Park on the Columbia River. The campground was beautiful, and downtown Portland was only about seven miles away. He had decided to visit Washington Park in Portland while he was there. He thought he might as well do some sightseeing while he wasn't busy concentrating on his next target.

When Doug arrived at the campground in the early evening, he set up his motor home, had a sandwich and milk with a few cookies, and just relaxed. He wanted a good night's sleep before going after his next target. It was hard to sleep; he kept rewinding the mosque's explosion in Seattle repeatedly in his mind.

After reading about Portland having six Hamas sympathizers convicted of conspiring with Hamas to plot against targets both in America and abroad, Doug wanted it to be his next target. He had read about a suspected terrorist training camp twenty-five miles outside Portland. He didn't know exactly where it was, but he would find out. The training camp was near a little town called Blain, Oregon, about fifty miles east of Klamath Falls. About a dozen Muslim men had been seen by a resident taking target practice several times. According to authorities, they thought the site had been abandoned, but he would find out for sure.

The next day, Doug was again on the hunt for his target. He unhooked his Mercedes and headed into downtown Portland. He wasn't going to leave Portland until he found the terrorist training camp. He tried his luck again with the homeless people on the streets of downtown Portland, and after talking to several of them and getting the same answer, he couldn't pinpoint the camp's exact location.

Finally, one of the guys said, "Go talk to someone in Blain, and they'll be able to tell you what you want to know."

Doug thanked him for the information and gave him a few bucks as he turned, walked away, and headed in Blain's direction.

When he got there, it didn't take long to find the general location of the camp. The people in town were aware of it and unhappy about it being there. The area was a secluded wooded area about ten miles out of town.

It took Doug some time to find the exact spot the terrorists were using; it was hidden deep in the woods, away from the main road. When he arrived at the location, there was no one around. There was a gate with a lock to the entrance and no way to drive into the place. After surveying the area for a few hours, he drove back into town, went to a local mosque, and picked up some pamphlets that the local Muslim organizations were distributing. Because he was fluent in Arabic, he read the information and told them about their next meeting and what type of meeting they were having.

It didn't seem suspicious, but he knew he had to spend some time in Portland to find out what and where his next target would be. He didn't want to blow up another mosque at that point. He desperately wanted to hit the terrorist training camp where they had tested their weapons. After a few days of searching, he found that the Muslim group was using the training camp he had been to a couple of times per week. He decided this was his next target.

Saturday morning, Doug woke up, grabbed his camera, jumped in his car, and headed to the Rose Gardens and the Japanese Gardens in Portland to spend the day walking around and taking pictures. As he strolled through the Gardens, he thought about Michael and his next target.

Sunday evening after dark, he took six of the I.E.D. s and placed them under his seat, along with the entrenching tool. He then headed for his target, and when he got there, he parked his car about a quarter of a mile away in the woods, hidden out of sight. He carried the I.E.D. s and the entrenching tool in the black metal detector bag and slowly reached the shooting range. He picked out several spots around the camp's parking area, dug holes, and meticulously planted his I.E.D. s with their pressure plates attached. When he planted them, he ensured the spots looked as natural as possible. He returned to his car, put the black bag and entrenching tool under his back seat, and drove back to his campsite. He bedded down for the night, knowing that his bombs had been planted and just waiting for their intended targets to arrive.

The following day, Doug had breakfast, packed everything up, checked out of the campsite, and headed back to Visalia. On the way home, he listened to news reports on the radio, but there wasn't anything about Portland's attacks. He stopped in Redding on his way home and spent a few hours sleeping and taking pictures of Mt. Shasta before driving to Visalia. When he got home, he unhooked his car and put everything away.

He could finally sit down and listen to the news again. CNN news reported several destroyed cars and six Muslim men were killed near Blain, Oregon. A few others were wounded from what appeared to be I.E.D.s like the ones used in Afghanistan and Iraq. The report said that it appeared they had been placed in a remote parking area that Muslims used for target practice. The report also said the Seattle attack seemed different but had some similarities to Portland's bomb material. It said that when the police and firefighters arrived at the mosque in Seattle and finally had everything under control, they found terrorist types of pamphlets, leaflets, and other material inside the mosque that said horrible things about killing Jewish and Christian people.

Doug was happy because he had accomplished his goal of killing some enemy terrorists and exposing their terrorist motives. He was sitting at home almost a thousand miles away, having a glass of red wine and feeling very satisfied with what he had done. When he later went into the bathroom, he got a look at himself in the mirror, and he had a substantial angry look on his face as he gritted his teeth and smiled. He entered Michael's room and said aloud, "At least I got a few of them, Michael. I promise I'll get a lot more for you. My mission has just begun."

He called Randy the following day to let him know he was home. He spent a week returning to his old routine of making more I.E.D. s and reading more information on Muslim Terrorist organizations.

* * *

Chapter 10 - San Francisco and Santa Clara

While at home, Doug tried to read as much material as possible regarding his following targets. One of the articles he read outraged him when it said that indoctrination was taking place in America's schools. Of significance was a report regarding seventh-grade world history textbooks. The report noted that many of the seventh-grade curricula in America follow the lead of California schools. Some schools in California require students to receive instructions and engage in activities to learn about Islamic history, culture, the Qur'an, and the religious practices of Muslims.

He read an article in the San Francisco Chronicle where an author said, "Islamists have taken what's come to be known as the "soft jihad" into America's classrooms, and children in K-12 are the casualties." The writer believed America was under assault, textbooks, curriculum, classroom exercises, film screenings, speakers, or teacher training in public education. (10) Doug couldn't believe what he was reading. He thought that America needed to open its eyes to what is being taught to our children. He thought, how could these Muslim people have this much influence in America to have it being taught in our school system?

Doug found three major mosques in San Francisco and seven in Santa Clara during his research. He just had to find the ones with suspected ties to the Muslim terrorist organizations, and they would be his following targets. He wanted to make sure he didn't just go in and kill many innocent men, women, and children by taking out the wrong mosque. He soon found that local authorities had criticized two mosques for handing out leaflets and other material regarding their disapproval of the Jews and Christians. They were going to be the two targets he was going to spend his focus on.

Doug loaded everything he needed under the back seat of his car and left at about 6:00 a.m. He didn't take his motor home this time because both targets were only a three-and-a-half-hour drive away. He had a lot of time to think about what he would do and was already planning his strategy and every move. He would first check in at the Mark Hopkins Hotel in San Francisco, where he would stay. It's located in San Francisco's heart and is a perfect spot to blend in with the rest of the tourists in the area.

Doug didn't have to go very far because his first target was only about six blocks from where he stayed. He checked around for a good parking area and looked to see the foot traffic near the mosque. This mosque was nothing like the one in Seattle. It sat back off the street about fifteen feet, and there was a covered "patio type" area that covered the entire front of the building, all the way to the street. He had a few problems with this target. One was that all the buildings on the road were attached, with no space between them. He knew he couldn't blow up the one building without the connecting buildings. The other problem he had was that everything was concrete, and there was no place to bury a bomb. He kept thinking, where can I place the bomb so it won't be seen? After surveying the covered area, he saw two large potted green plants on the patio. He believed that would be the place where he would bury the C-4 bomb.

Once satisfied with this target, Doug drove to his next target, forty miles south of Santa Clara, to check it out. The building had a flat roof and was in a commercial neighborhood downtown. The building had an alley in the back, so Doug drove around to the building's rear. He wanted to see if there was any way he could get onto the roof without being seen. He saw an air conditioning unit next to an access rail that he could climb up on and climb to the building's upper part. He figured the top of the building was the best spot to place his bomb.

Satisfied with his plan, he drove back to San Francisco to the Mark Hopkins hotel. After arriving, he went into the restaurant and had lunch. Then he went up to his room to relax for a few hours. He would go back after dark and check out his targets to see what activity was happening.

The next day, Doug put on his Muslim disguise, went to his first stop in San Francisco, and slowly walked up to the mosque door. One of the men standing outside acknowledged him in Arabic as he looked Doug up and down. Doug said, "Hello," back to him in Arabic. Then he asked the man if it was okay to go inside. The man didn't say anything; he nodded his head.

Doug walked in the door, slowly looked around, and saw familiar pamphlets and books on a fold-out table at the back of the room. As he picked up one of the pamphlets, he could tell it was full of propaganda, just like others he had seen and heard. He didn't take the time to read it all. He just put it back down, turned to the man he had spoken to, and asked, "Can you please tell me when the next meeting is?" The man quietly told him the next big meeting would be in a few days at 8 p.m.

With his arms folded behind his back, Doug thanked him and returned to the entrance. He had seen and heard everything he needed to know about this mosque. He checked out the potted plants as he stood on the porch. He wanted to make sure he could plant the C-4 bomb in one of them. As he left, he was proud of himself for feeling so comfortable blending in with the rest of the Muslim men.

Doug decided on his second target. It didn't matter when they would have their next meeting; he would attack it on the same night as the San Francisco mosque. Doug hoped there would be some terrorists in the building when he set off the explosion. He returned to his car, removed his disguise, and put it back under the back seat. He then returned to the hotel and his room to shower and change into nice clothes. He wanted to relax and rest for the evening, so he went to the "Top of the Mark" for dinner. He didn't want to let his mission consume him and take complete control of his emotions.

The following day, he was up early but just hung out in his room and relaxed for a while before he walked down to the Pier side Restaurant at Fisherman's Wharf. He wanted to have clam chowder and fish and chips for lunch. It was a couple of miles of walking, but he felt he could use the exercise. As he walked along the street near the water, many amateur acts were performed along the sidewalks. He thought many of them were clever and others just plain ridiculous. One act that had gotten to Shirley the last time they were there was the guy that jumps out at you with a bush covering his body. Doug thought it was so ridiculous but clever. He didn't know why but remembered tipping the guy five bucks.

As Doug walked along, he heard a man shouting something as people walked by. Doug moved closer to see if he could listen to the young man's words. When he got within ten feet of him, he could tell that he was in his mid-twenties or early thirties and said that the Jews and the Christians were the world's problems. They were the cause of the war in Iraq and Afghanistan. He was a Caucasian man, a little overweight, with stringy, long brown hair, a mustache, and a beard. He wore a tan shirt with loose-fitting slacks, a dark brown corduroy vest, and old white tennis shoes, and he said other derogatory things about how the American troops were killing Muslim children in Iraq and Afghanistan.

It sent Doug into a quiet but controlled rage when he heard that. He could tell his face was red because he could feel the blood rush to his head as he thought, this is the typical outspoken, anti-American guy I want to destroy. I must find a way to silence this jerk for good. He is no better than the other terrorist spreading their lies and hatred worldwide. After watching him for a few minutes and becoming angrier by the minute, he decided to walk down to the Pier side Restaurant where he could relax and have lunch.

While Doug was in the restaurant, he couldn't take his mind off the guy in the street. He began to plan his strategy for how he could kill him. He remembered that he had brought two syringes full of Potassium Chloride with him. He had decided that if he were ever caught by law enforcement, he would use one of them on himself. After lunch, he returned to the hotel, got the syringe, and returned to the Wharf. The guy was still spouting his hatred and lies when he got there.

He browsed around the stores in the area for a few hours and kept an eye on the loudmouth the entire time. Finally, the guy must have decided he had done his just part for the Muslim terrorist organizations for the day and started to leave. Doug followed him from a safe distance until he walked down a somewhat secluded street to his car. As Doug got close to him, he looked around to make sure no one was nearby or watching what was about to happen.

When the guy opened his car door and sat down, Doug quickly walked up behind him and held the door open with the left side of his hip and left leg. He hadn't noticed what Doug had done as he leaned back in his seat and started to shut the car door. Doug stuck him in the back of the neck with the needle and pushed in the deadly substance. His last words as he felt the needle's prick go deep into his neck were, "Hey, what did you do to me?" Doug didn't say anything to him; he just shut the car door with his leg and quickly walked away. When he glanced back, he saw the loudmouth slumped over in his seat. As he walked briskly back to the hotel, he thought that poor fool wouldn't instigate any more of his hatred and lies.

That night, Doug waited until around 3:00 am and then went to Santa Clara and quietly made his way onto the mosque's top and planted the C-4 bomb and detonator. A vent had a round rotating cover made of sheet metal, and Doug removed it, gently lowered the bomb into the dark hole, and put the cover back into the vent. He wore his disguise when he was through and returned to San Francisco's mosque. He had the C-4 bomb hidden under his dark, loose-fitting coat as he approached the building. He approached his target slowly, and when he was confident no one was around, he dug out the soil around the base of one of the large plants and quickly hid his bomb. He covered it and made sure it looked undisturbed before he left.

The following day he made plans with the concierge at Mark Hopkins to see them play "Phantom of the Opera" the following evening. He told the concierge he wanted to attend the late show at 10:00 pm. That would give him time to clean up after blowing up his two targets. The play was at the local playhouse theater downtown. He and Shirley had seen the "Phantom of the Opera" in New York when they stayed at the Waldorf Hotel in May of 2001, and they both loved it. He could still see Shirley as the tears welled in her eyes and how she tried so hard not to cry during one of the play's sad scenes.

The next day, he took pictures of San Francisco and the famous Sea Lions near the pier. He wanted an early dinner before he exploded his targets, so he had dinner around 5:30 p.m. Soon after dinner, he headed to Santa Clara. By then, it was dark, and he was surprised by all the activity at the mosque as he drove by his target. Doug drove down the street several blocks and put on his disguise. He also put on the remote-control detonator and slowly walked toward the mosque. As soon as he was within range, he pushed the button, and the explosion went off. When it went off, he ducked, turned, and started walking back to his car, forcing himself not to run. He was both nervous and excited on his way back to San Francisco.

Once he returned to San Francisco, he parked his car and walked toward his next target. When he got within striking distance of the mosque, he pushed the detonator. The mosque people were in the middle of their meeting when the bomb went off. And it shook all the buildings in the area, and everything burst into flames. The blast was so large that it destroyed the mosque and a few connecting buildings. He was about a hundred yards away, and tiny debris landed in the street and around him. For a moment, he thought, that's ironic. Now I'm going to get hit by pieces of my bomb. He dodged a few falling pieces as he went to his car.

Doug was pleased that he had gotten his two targets. He drove several blocks away into a secluded area, then took off his disguise and put it back under his back seat. He returned to the Mark Hopkins, went to his room, showered, and dressed for the opera. Now that the two targets were blown up, he tried to put them out of his mind for the moment, just like he had done with the targets in Vietnam. No matter how he tried, he couldn't help himself; he kept thinking about what had happened to Michael and how he had died. The pain of that loss was haunting him, and he would not let him rest.

The following day, he packed and left before noon, and he was back in Visalia around three in the afternoon. Once there, he put everything away and lay on the couch for a few hours to unwind. He was mentally and physically exhausted from all the planning and excitement of taking out his targets.

Later that evening, he made a sandwich, poured himself milk, and went into the living room to listen to the news reports. The attacks on Santa Clara and San Francisco were on the evening news. The reports said twenty-two Muslims had been killed in the San Francisco attack and twelve wounded. Eleven had died in the Santa Clara attack, and nine were wounded. Doug scoffed as he thought, "Yea, I also got a bonus with the loudmouth jerk on the sidewalk." Even though it didn't make the news report one of his kills, he was satisfied knowing he had done his part in getting that terrorist off the street. He wasn't feeling any remorse for what he had done. He was getting a great deal of satisfaction for avenging Michael's death.

Law enforcement agencies found leaflets and other materials in the two mosques about killing the "Jews and the Christians." Printed on some of the material, in boldface print, it said things like, "It is our duty to destroy all infidels and destroy the west." The news reported that the law enforcement community had difficulty figuring out what person or organization was responsible for the bombings. Because of the similarities, law enforcement strongly believed these two crimes had to be connected to Portland and Seattle's attacks. Doug was somewhat offended that they called them crimes because he didn't consider his actions crimes; he viewed his "victims" as casualties of war, and when it's war, it's not a crime, just like his Captain had told him so many years ago. As he watched, he shouted at the television, "Come on, America; I've declared war on all these terrorist organizations. Open your eyes; they must be stopped before it's too late."

The next day, he did his usual chores and returned to making bombs. He needed a few weeks before he hit his following targets in Los Angeles and San Diego. He would wait until he felt the timing was right for him before going on his subsequent attacks.

* * *

Chapter 11 - The Fresno Leader

Much to Doug's surprise, during his research, he found that in Fresno, California, there was a leader of a local Muslim mosque who, in the past, had openly made threats against Israel and the United States. He had spoken his hatred of the Jewish people to his congregation. Once he learned this information, Doug visited the Fresno mosque to learn more about this radical leader. He was angry that this leader had made threats against the Jewish and Christian people, and his mosque was only a forty-five-minute drive from his hometown.

The leader was in his late sixties with long gray hair, a long gray beard, and a mustache. He was about five feet six inches tall and a little overweight. His mosque had a considerable following in the Fresno area. Because of his open dislike for the Christian and Jewish people, Doug wanted to see who he was and how easy it would be to kill him. The mosque was located south of Fresno and on the outskirts of town. It was surrounded by grape vineyards and had a main road in front of the mosque just off the main freeway.

When Doug first arrived at the mosque, he drove past it until he was about a quarter-mile away and parked in one of the vineyards. A dirt avenue road separated the owner's vineyards from each other, and he had a good view of the mosque from that location. His car was hidden between a row of vines. He took out his binoculars and observed the mosque's activity from his vehicle for a few minutes. There wasn't much going on, so he thought he would do more research and see when they had their meetings. Doug went to a local library and used the computer. He soon found a picture of the leader from his gathered information, so he knew what he looked like. During one of their meetings, he returned and sat in his car in the mosque parking lot to observe and wait to identify his next target. He could easily spot the leader when he arrived at the mosque, so now that he was convinced he knew who he was, he decided he would return another time and kill him.

Doug found out when they had a weekly meeting, so before the session started, Doug returned to the same spot in the vineyard where he had been a few days earlier. He got out of his car, retrieved his rifle from under the back seat, loaded it, and found a firing position on the ground. He left the trunk open just a little so he could quickly hide his rifle once he was finished killing the leader. The spot he had chosen had grape vines every twelve feet apart, and he could hide but simultaneously have a clear view of the mosque down the middle of the vineyard row. He lay down in a prone firing position on the ground and set up his rifle with its tripod and scope aimed in the mosque's direction. He ensured he wore his surgical gloves and booties that covered his shoes and disguise this time.

Doug waited patiently for his target as the mosque started getting activity. Soon, his target arrived, and he could tell it was the leader because everyone was paying so much attention to him. To be sure he didn't kill the wrong man, he spotted him with the rifle scope, and it was him. He took careful aim, let out his breath, and zeroed in on his target's chest. He slowly squeezed the trigger when the crosshairs were in the middle of his chest. The rifle let out a little "puff" sound as it fired, and a dash of smoke left the rifle as the bullet hit its target. Doug said softly, "I got you, sucker." He didn't wait to see if he had killed the leader; he immediately grabbed the discharged cartridge and put his rife in the trunk. He was out of there in just a matter of a few seconds. He drove on a few country roads before he caught freeway 99, heading south to Visalia. It happened so fast that he felt it was over and was gone before anyone realized what had just happened to their leader.

The next day, as he watched the local news channels, they reported that a sniper had killed a Muslim leader at his Fresno mosque. The news anchors said that law enforcement officials were wondering who could be responsible for killing the leader. They speculated that the FBI and other law enforcement agencies would probably have to be called to help search for the killer. Doug couldn't help but think good luck with that one. All he knew was that this leader wouldn't spread any more of his hatred and propaganda to his congregation.

* * *

Chapter 12 - San Diego and Los Angeles

While home, Doug turned his attention to his following two targets. He started reading everything he could about the San Diego and Los Angeles mosques. He found sixteen Muslim Mosques in San Diego alone, and although some have suspected ties to Hamas and the Algerian Islamic Group, one stuck out in Doug's mind that he wanted to target. The leader of the mosque is an American-born Iranian Muslim named Aftell Taldo-allid. He is in his mid to late forties, tall and thin. He has long black and gray hair, a black and gray beard, and a mustache. He is well-dressed and very articulate in his speeches to the public and members of his mosque.

For several years, the FBI and CIA have proclaimed that Taldo-allied has suspected ties to Hamas and sent money to the Hamas organization in Palestine. He has made numerous trips to Palestine, but the FBI and CIA have not tied the money flow direction from him or his mosque to the Hamas organization. Doug found that he is on the most-watched list of the CIA and FBI. He decided he would target just the one individual leader in San Diego instead of an entire mosque. He believed that if he could kill the mosque leader, it might slow them down from sending money to the terrorist organizations in Palestine and bring the FBI in to investigate his mosque.

In a 2004 press release, it was announced, "Hamas considers the U.S. as an enemy and an accomplice to the Israeli enemy aggression against the Palestinians." It said, "The U.S. will face responsibility for its position as an accomplice with Israel." In America, the Hamas organization has been aided by bogus charities and organizations sympathizing with the Palestinian cause. In 2008, the United States finally declared Hamas a terrorist organization. (17)

There were tons of mosques in the Los Angeles area, but Doug wanted to blow up the Omir Del Al-Panton Mosque in western Los Angeles. The United States government has criticized this mosque as spreading leaflets and other material that said, "Kill the Jews and Christians." Because of their outright call to kill Americans, they were Doug's number one target in Los Angeles. In 2004, a Foundation based in Saudi Arabia with branch offices in the United States, which this mosque supported, had its assets blocked by the FBI after finding that it was directly funding al-Qaeda.

A few days passed, and Doug was on his way to San Diego to visit his target, Taldo-allied. He knew what Taldo-all looked like and where his mosque was located. When he arrived in San Diego, he knew he would stay at the bay's Bahia Resort Hotel for a few days. They had an excellent ferry boat that takes you across the bay to Old Town San Diego. He had taken the ferry boat once before with Shirley some years ago when he was at a physician's conference. Like the last trip to San Francisco, it wasn't the same without Shirley. Once he arrived, he checked in under a fake name and gave the clerk enough cash to cover extras he might need.

After he settled into his room and was comfortable with everything, he decided to check out the mosque and see if he could find out anything he needed to know about his target. He drove to the mosque, and after being there several hours, he spotted the leader. He thought he would wait, follow him home, and maybe kill him at that location.

Once Taldo-allied was finished for the day, Doug followed from a safe distance, but Doug drove past it a few blocks when he arrived home. He watched as Taldo-allied pushed his garage button, drove into the garage, and quickly shut the door behind him. His house was on a hill across the road from a city park. Doug thought this would be a perfect place to take out Taldo-allied with his sniper rifle.

The park was about two hundred yards wide and four hundred yards long. He parked his car on the other side of the park and walked along slowly until he found a clear view of Taldo-allid's house. The park seemed to be busy with joggers and walkers, and because of all the activity going on in the park, Doug thought he would have to shoot him at night. He would be a difficult target since he parked his car in the garage.

After studying the location and contemplating the options, he thought, this isn't work; the risk is too high, and the chances of hitting him are too small. I wouldn't have enough time to site in my rifle and kill him before he was in his garage and the door was closed.

Doug drove back to the mosque to view the surrounding areas and see where he could set up another firing position. Because the economy had been so bad the past couple of years, a few commercial buildings were about a quarter-mile away, which were not occupied and for rent. He decided to try to remove Taldo-allied from the top of the roof of one of those vacant buildings.

There was an alley that ran down the back of the buildings. It would be easy to shoot his target and escape in his car. He found a place with easy access to the roof, so he decided this was the best spot. Once satisfied with his choice, he left and returned to the hotel to relax for the evening.

The following night, Doug wore his black pullover sweatshirt and baseball cap. When he arrived at the vacant building, he parked his car in the alley, grabbed his rifle, crept to the top, and took up his shooting position. He sat hidden on the roof and waited for Taldo-allied to leave the mosque. He waited patiently, fighting the cold night air, and as soon as Taldo-allied stepped out of the mosque, Doug had an aim at him and fired. The bullet hit him in the middle of the chest, and he immediately went to the ground.

Doug hadn't noticed a man walking on the other side of the street across from him. As soon as he heard the puff of Doug's rifle, he yelled something at Doug. In a short second, Doug pointed his rifle at him as if he were going to shoot him. The man took off running when he saw the weapon pointed at him. Doug immediately grabbed the spent cartridge and scurried down the walls of the building. He threw his rifle in the back seat of his car and took off.

After driving a few miles to a secluded area, he got out and put his rifle under the back seat. He removed the sweatshirt and baseball cap and put them under the back seat. On the way back to the hotel, he wondered what the witness might say to law enforcement when he talked to them. He knew it was too dark and too far away for the witness to describe him in much detail.

He was shaking from the excitement as he drove back to his hotel and showered. After getting dressed and relaxed, he rode on the ferry boat to Old Town. He was still thinking about Taldo-allied and the witness who had seen him. He sat on the ferry boat deep in thought and wondered how Michael might feel about what he was doing. He said, "I guess now it doesn't matter, Michael, the mission to destroy the terrorists has begun." He rode across to Old Town, had a nice quiet dinner alone, and then ferried back to his hotel a few hours later. No matter how hard he tried, he couldn't shake the anger and loneliness deep in his heart.

The following day, Doug checked out of the Bahia Hotel and headed to West Los Angeles to reach his next target. He got a room at the Hilton Hotel at Universal Studios. He figured it would be a good cover for him, and it was several miles from his next target. Again, he checked in under a fake name and paid in cash.

It was about a thirty-minute drive to the mosque he wanted to blow up, and there was a lot of activity when he arrived. Walking around in his Muslim disguise, he began talking with the people, and soon, he knew this was the correct target. He spent about thirty minutes looking around and talking with some men standing around. He finally spotted a place he believed he could plant a bomb without it being seen.

Satisfied with his decision, he returned to his hotel, waited until late that night, and drove back to the mosque. No one was around, so he took the bomb from under his clothes and planted it in the dirt under one of the front windows.

The next day, Doug spent the entire day at Universal Studios, just taking in all the activities and trying his hardest to enjoy himself. It all had empty meaning to him, no matter how hard he tried. Around 3:00 p.m., he returned to his room and napped for a few hours before having an early dinner in the hotel restaurant.

When he returned to the Mosque later that evening, a lot was happening there. He had once again put on his disguise and walked toward the mosque. When he got within range of his terrorist target, he pushed the button, and the mosque exploded in a ball of fire. He just turned and calmly walked back to his car. He drove to a secluded area, removed the disguise, and put everything under his back seat. Now, his two targets had been blown up. His mission in San Diego and Los Angeles was completed.

The following morning, Doug checked out of the hotel and drove back to Visalia. To his knowledge, no one knew he had been gone for five days. Once home, he put everything away and took his rifle into his shop to ensure he cleaned it before using it again. He finally relaxed as he sat down and turned on CNN and FOX news stations to see what they were reporting. He flipped from one channel to the next to see if there was any information about the attacks.

The news reported that fifteen Muslims were killed at the Los Angeles mosque, and fourteen were wounded. Of course, there was an uproar over the Muslim leader in San Diego. After watching some of the Muslim protests, he thought some people in America might have thought the leader he killed was some excellent, upstanding patriot of America. If so, they didn't know the man's real goals like the FBI and CIA did. He knew the more law enforcement dug into the material they found at the exploded mosque in Los Angeles. More information would come out about the actual Muslim terrorist activity that was going on inside the mosque walls.

Whenever Doug went into Michael's room and looked around, the more he missed Michael and the more he felt justified in the mission he was on of his act of vengeance. Soon, some news agencies called him the "American Terrorist." They still didn't know if it was an individual or a group of people targeting Muslim organizations. All they knew was that a terrorist was blowing up mosques and killing Muslim people in America. Doug didn't feel like these were loving Muslim people; he was convinced they were terrorists.

Doug spent about two weeks packing his motor home and preparing everything to leave Visalia permanently to continue his mission in other parts of America. He went to the bank and pulled out a large amount of cash, destroyed the hard drive to his computer, and ensured he got rid of any evidence, including books, magazines, pamphlets, and anything resembling Muslim or terrorist information. He made several more bombs and removed all the bomb-making material from the shop. He vacuumed every inch of the building to ensure there was no evidence or residue anywhere to be found. He dumped the vacuum bag and contents in the trash bin several miles away and put a new bag in the vacuum cleaner a few days before he left.

He called Michael's best friend Gary and told him that he had given Michael's Ford Mustang to him because Michael wanted him to have it. Doug didn't have any use for it now that Michael was gone. He had Gary meet him the following day at his house, and he signed over the title. Gary was both excited but sad because this was the vehicle he and Michael had shared so many good times. Doug told him he would take his motor home and see different parts of America.

He wished Gary well and said, "Thanks for being such a good friend to Michael and me over the years." Gary was so choked up that he could only nod to thank him. He shook Doug's hand and hugged him before he left.

When he was convinced he had everything he needed, he met with Randy and Karen and gave them the keys to the house and shop. He also signed the title to Randy's boat since he had no more use for it.

Randy didn't know what was going on with Doug, but he thanked him and said, "Take care of yourself, brother, and we will see you when we see you. Just remember that I love you."

Doug said, "I love you too, brother," as they hugged, shook hands, and said their good-byes.

As he was leaving, Doug finally broke down the following day and cried. He went into his bedroom, knelt, and told Shirley how much he loved her. He then walked into Michael's room to say goodbye. It was a room that he had gotten very acquainted with over the past few months. He had several one-way conversations with Michael in the room since he was killed.

Even though this had been Doug's home for many years, his strong desire to fulfill his war against the radical Muslim terrorist organizations outweighed his desire to stay. He had tears in his eyes as he looked over at the house from the motor home for the last time. He reached down and rubbed Michael's dog tags hanging from his neck. He had the motor home loaded down, and his Mercedes was in tow as he quietly said good-bye and pulled away.

* * *

Chapter 13 – Doug's on a Mission

Doug was heading to the southern part of the United States to locate some of his targets and blow them up. Once he blew up a few of them in the South, he would then head north to throw off the FBI, CIA, or any other law enforcement agencies that would be looking for him. He also knew many targets in the northeastern United States that he wanted to blow up. He knew the great thing about being in a motor home and older was that he fit right in with the rest of the "baby boomers," who were using their RVs to travel across America. As he drove along, he wondered if anyone would ever suspect an older retired doctor as a terrorist.

What was unique to Doug is that none of the terrorist organizations had ever coordinated their worldwide efforts with other terrorist groups until they came to the United States and set up their organizations in America. He firmly believed it was the goal of the radical Muslim organizations of the world to take over America someday. He wondered if the everyday hard-working Americans even knew about the presence of thousands of Muslim Mosques already spread throughout America.

Doug was targeting first place in South Carolina, and it is called "Holy Islamtown." The town's founder was well-known in the world of radical Islam. A revolutionary leader established the first Muslim Holy Shrine in America at "Holy Islamtown" in 1983. According to some reports from the local people who lived near Islamtown, it is home to hundreds of Muslims in Islamic attire. Most members drive late-model SUVs with license plates from Pennsylvania, New Jersey, New York, Ohio, South Carolina, and Tennessee. The locals say some members work as toll booth operators for the New York State Thruway.

In contrast, others are employed at a credit card processing center that maintains Americans' confidential financial records.

The locals have said they hear bursts of gunfire all the time and know there is some military training going on in Holy Islamtown. One local said, "They are training for war, either for war here in this country or against our troops in Iraq or Afghanistan." One neighbor said he saw an armed guard carrying an AK47, and another said she saw men carrying M16s in the town. Locals believed that when the time was right and their terrorist leaders ordered them to attack, they would attack America from within. They were already armed, so Doug wondered who could stop them unless it was the National Guard or our military. (24)

The lack of concern by the local law enforcement agencies floored Doug. According to the reports, local law enforcement has taken the stance that unless these people threaten themselves or the local people, they leave them alone. Doug would take his time getting to his next target and gather his thoughts because he had to do some serious planning as he traveled east across America on Highway 10.

Before he got to his target, Doug decided to take some time and get his mind off his mission for a while. He knew that if he did proper planning, it would be better and more accessible for him, and maybe he could cut down on mistakes he had made in some of his previous attacks.

His first stop was the breathtaking Grand Canyon. He was going to Sedona, Arizona, and took the historic railway South Rim Grand Canyon tour. It was an eleven-hour tour by rail starting in Sedona and ending up back at Sedona. The train has stops along the way to walk part of the south rim trail and visit the Grand Canyon Village. He felt the ride's cost would be worth it since he had never been close to the Grand Canyon. He found a spot to park his motor home for the day and take the shuttle to the rail. He was a little excited that he would get some great pictures. He spent the entire day doing the tour and had dinner at the local Sedona Hotel Restaurant.

The following day, he was back on the road again. On his second stop, he wanted to go a little out of his way off route ten and make sure he visited the Vietnam Veterans Memorial in the Sangre de Cristo Mountains in northern New Mexico. He had read about it and wanted very much to see it. The memorial was initially constructed on the Val Verde Ranch in Moreno Valley by the Doctor Victor Westphal family in honor of their son David Westphal, killed by enemy gunfire in South Vietnam in 1968. It tore at Doug's heart that a grieving family had loved their son so much that they built such a remarkable memorial in honor of him. Once there, he was taken aback by the monument and spent several hours taking pictures and reading everything regarding the memorial. Before he left the memorial, he said a silent prayer to all the fallen American soldiers and Michael.

As he made his way east, he wanted to see the Oklahoma Memorial in downtown Oklahoma City on his third stop. The memorial was built in honor of the one hundred and sixty-eight people killed and six hundred and eighty wounded by a homegrown American terrorist, Timothy McVeigh, in 1995. McVeigh had parked a Rider rental truck filled with explosives in front of the Alfred P. Murray federal building on April 19, 1995, and blew it up. Doug always believed that McVeigh didn't act alone and was part of a radical Muslim terrorist organization. On the outside of each gate leading into the memorial, they bear this inscription:

"We come here to remember those who were killed, those who survived, and those who changed forever. May all who leave here know the impact of violence. May this memorial offer comfort, strength, peace, hope, serenity."

When Doug saw this memorial, he felt very angry with the terrorist McVeigh and sad for all the people who lost their lives and the people who lost their loved ones at the hands of this home-grown madman.

He wondered what made a man like McVeigh want to kill hundreds of his fellow Americans. Doug knew why he was on his mission against the terrorist, but what was McVeigh's motivation? Seeing this memorial just strengthened his resolve to continue his fight against the terrorist organizations in America, especially American-born homegrown terrorists.

He had never seen Nashville, Tennessee, or Branson, Missouri, so his next stops along his journey would be both places. He wanted to take pictures and see some of the live entertainment. He didn't have any Missouri targets he wanted to go after, so he passed through this state. He loved country music, especially by Vince Gill and Reba McIntyre. When he was a few days out from Branson, he called and made reservations at the K.O.A. campground. He loved this country and all the beautiful trees and lush green wooded areas. The further south he got, the friendlier the people seemed to get. He loved "Southern Hospitality."

This campground was only a few miles from downtown, and all the entertainment was done there. They had full hookups, cable television, and a shuttle bus that took people to the shows if they booked the show through the park. Once he had checked in and had everything settled, he thought he would make a reservation to see one famous country and Western concert. George Strait was performing the night he wanted to go. It was a dinner show, and it worked out perfectly for him. He had a nice dinner and a few glasses of red wine. Even though he was alone, he thought it felt good not to relax. During this brief time, he wasn't thinking about the terrorists; he enjoyed himself for the first time in a long time.

* * *

Chapter 14 - South Carolina

When Doug woke up the next day, he was refreshed and ready to seek his next target. Exiting the motor home and getting some fresh air, he stretched his arms and said, "Islamtown, here I come." He ensured his car was hooked up, and everything was ready to go, and then he headed to the K.O.A. campground in South Carolina. It was about forty miles from his target of Islamtown.

Once he got to the campground and set up his camp, he spent the next few days just checking out the terrorist camp. He knew if this camp had armed guards, he would have to use what he had learned in his Army training years ago to root them out. He would have to take a more offensive approach while assaulting the camp. He hid in the woods and watched the armed guards as they patrolled the camp's perimeter. He thought this looked more like a prison to me, except they aren't trying to keep people from getting out; they protect it from people coming in.

That area of South Carolina is wooded; to keep from being caught, he would have to wear the camouflaged uniform. He knew he could take out targets from a safe distance with his sniper rifle, and it would be hard for them to spot him. His biggest concern was he would get the attention of the FBI, CIA, and other law enforcement agencies.

The next day, he drove into the woods, put on his Muslim disguise, and then drove to a local shopping center and parked his Mercedes. He walked about two miles to a rental company and rented a car. He gave them his fake name and soon had the car. He drove to Islamtown camp and found his way to the main entrance. Just as he was about to enter, an armed and uniformed guard stopped him at the gate. The guard was a big, well-built African American man, and he asked Doug about the nature of his business in Islamtown. He told the guard he was looking for his brother from Kabul. He didn't know if the guard believed him because he asked if he could search his car before entering. Doug thought I'm sure glad I didn't bring my Mercedes. Doug looked up at him and said, sure, that would be okay with him. After the guard scoured his car and was satisfied he was not a threat to the compound, he let him pass.

While driving around the camp, armed, uniformed guards stopped him several times. They again asked him what he was doing driving around the compound. Each time he told them he was looking for his brother from Kabul, they let him continue.

Doug drove around the area for a while and had an excellent idea of the compound's size. He also found where the guards were located. He also found where the people of the camp spent their time during the day. He knew he couldn't get close to the high-profile areas and place a bomb because they would search his car. Also, it was too risky to try to get into the compound on foot because of the guards.

He decided he would have to use his sniper rifle and take out some guards from outside the perimeter. He devised a plan to set up an area outside the perimeter about two hundred yards and move in a circular clockwise pattern. He would kill as many armed guards as possible with his sniper rifle. He wanted to end up on the other side of the hill, where he would leave his rental car and make his escape. He knew that once he started shooting the guards, the woods would be full of them coming after him. He thought this would be an excellent time to carry his pistol if one of the guards got too close.

Doug drove back to his Mercedes, got his rifle, pistol, and ammunition, and put them in the back of the rental car. He went downtown and had lunch. Later that day, he headed back to the terrorist compound in the rental car. He waited until just before dark and parked the car on the other side of the hill just like he had planned. He hiked back over the hill to his first target near the front gate. Once comfortable with that location, he got down in a prone position and zeroed in on his target. He let out his breath and slowly squeezed the trigger, shooting the first guard, and watched as he went down. The guard screamed out in pain and fired his weapon in the air. In just a few minutes, another guard came running to his aid. As soon as he got there, Doug shot him as well. Now, he had two guards down near the front gate.

He started following his plan and moving toward his car in a crouched and circular direction. As he made his way up and over the hill, he shot four more guards coming after him from inside the camp. As he got to the car, he breathed heavily from excitement. He was getting ready to put his rifle in the vehicle when another guard came running over the hill toward him. He was about a hundred yards away and firing wildly in Doug's direction with his automatic weapon. Doug quickly zeroed in on him, shot him, and watched as he went down. He then threw the rifle into the car and started to speed away.

When Doug reached the bottom of the hill, he saw a black SUV about a half-mile behind him, speeding toward him. He floored the rental car to escape the SUV, but it was coming after him quickly. As it got a little closer, he could tell two guys were in it, and the passenger had a gun sticking out the side window firing at his car. He had to decide quickly about what to do, or they would soon be on top of him. He couldn't outrun them in the rental car, so he had to come up with something fast. He thought, Doug, what a fine mess you got yourself into now. He saw a sharp turn in the road ahead and stepped on the gas to temporarily escape them.

He was about two hundred yards ahead of the SUV when he made the sharp turn, slowed down, and pulled the car over to the side of the road. He jumped out with his rifle and used the vehicle to support his shooting position. When the SUV started to make the turn and was only about fifty yards away, he quickly zeroed in on the passenger and shot him in the head. The driver slammed on his brakes, and the SUV slid to a stop as dust flew up in the air and temporarily covered the

SUV. Doug could tell the driver was trying to get to his rifle in his hands when the dust cleared. Doug took a shot and busted the front windshield but missed him. He quickly aimed, and his second bullet hit him in the head. As the driver slumped over the steering wheel, the SUV slowly drifted into the middle of the dirt road.

Doug didn't look back as he tossed his rifle on the car's passenger side and took off down the hill. He knew other guards would soon try to pursue him, so he didn't waste time getting out of there. He kept looking back through his rear-view mirror and the side mirrors to see if anyone was after him as he speeded back to town. Luckily, he had no more encounters with the guards on returning to town.

Once back in town, he drove the rental car to the shopping center, parked his Mercedes, and transferred everything back under the back seat. He quickly put on his Muslim disguise and drove the rental car back to the rental company. He parked it in front and left the keys inside. He walked back to the shopping center where he had parked his Mercedes, and before going directly to his car, he went into one of the stores to purchase something to look like he had been shopping. After his purchase, he calmly walked over to his Mercedes, removed his Muslim disguise, put it under the seat, got in the car, and left.

When Doug got back at camp and had time to reflect on everything that had happened on this mission, he was angry with himself because the guards chasing him in the SUV were not something he had planned to happen. He was disappointed that he had to leave the bullet casings in the woods for the law enforcement's first clue as to the type of rifle he used. He was not very comfortable with the entire way he handled this attack. It could've backfired on him very quickly. The guards in the SUV or other people from the compound could've trapped him. Maybe even by the police on their way to the compound. The only thing that may have saved him this time was that they weren't expecting this attack on their compound, and he caught them by surprise.

Even though he had done a lot of planning, he thought he might have been too eager to kill some of these terrorists instead of taking his time and spending a few more days checking it out. After much thought, he decided to take his time and be more careful before hitting his next target.

The following day, he reattached his vehicle to the motor home and was back on the road. According to the CNN news reports, he had killed eight men, six at the compound and two on the compound's small dirt road. He also wounded one guard. After his mistakes, he still felt like it was a successful mission. He knew the FBI, the CIA, and other law enforcement would come in and investigate what had happened. Maybe they would find out that the people in the compound were armed guards carrying automatic weapons. At the very least, his attack would bring attention to the suspected Islamtown terrorist compound.

If Doug's assumptions were correct, it would cause many more of the terrorist men to arm themselves and start carrying their guns into the streets of their compound. Hopefully, law enforcement officials would have to investigate why those people had weapons. Doug thought, what was so important that they had to carry guns to try and keep people out? Regardless, he had done his part and, in the process, killed eight more terrorists. He was happy he could get a few from this compound, which initially looked impossible to penetrate.

* * *

Chapter 15 - Dixie, Tennessee

Doug was heading to Nashville. It was a place he had always heard about and seen on television, and now he would see it in person. He made reservations at the Two Rivers Campground, just two miles from Opryland. It's a peaceful resort with full hook-up sites, laundry, a game room, a swimming pool, stores, and more. It also had a concierge desk to make reservations to whatever tourist attractions he wanted to see.

He wanted to see two things in Nashville while passing through: Elvis Presley's Graceland and the Grand Old Opry. Doug and Shirley had tried to get tickets a few times to watch Elvis perform live in Las Vegas, but they were always sold out before he could get them. Elvis was Shirley's favorite entertainer, and he always regretted not taking her to see him before he died in 1982. Now that he would be in Nashville, he knew he had to take a tour of Graceland.

While growing up, his dad loved the Grand Old Opry and would have the entire family watch it on television on Saturday nights. His love for Country and Western Music was instilled in his heart. On his way into Nashville, he saw a billboard saying Vince Gill would perform at the Grand Old Opry on Saturday night. She was one of his favorite singers, and he wanted to do his best to get a ticket to see the show.

After he arrived at his campsite, he set up his motor home, unhooked his car, and went to the concierge desk. He made reservations to tour Graceland and was lucky to get a ticket to see Vince Gill. He was ready to relax for a few days after his last attack. He spent the rest of the day relaxing around the motor home and doing laundry. Early the following day, he had to jump on a shuttle bus waiting next to the pool to go to Graceland. The tour lasted for several hours and included lunch. He took his camera along for a few pictures.

He thought about Shirley the entire time and wished she could've been with him.

The Saturday night show at the Grand Old Opry was even better than Doug expected. The dinner show came with two drinks of your choice and a nice prime rib dinner. He thought Vince Gill and the rest of the group put on a great show, just like the ones he watched on television as a kid. He was glad he had gotten the opportunity to be there and see them perform live.

His next target was in Dixie, Tennessee. It was about eighty miles from Nashville. According to the reports, Dixie has gradually become a stronghold for radical Islamic terrorist organizations transforming parts of Tennessee's state. It is the type of infiltration that Doug felt he had to stop or at least slow down. His new target was a sprawling closed camp with many mobile homes and several areas used for training in hand-to-hand combat, firing weapons, and using explosives. He had to plan carefully how he wanted to attack this camp. He wanted to try and blow up some of his terrorist targets while training or getting ready to train. Once he decided what to do, he put four - I.E.D. s under the seat of his Mercedes along with four - one-pound sticks of C-4, some wire, the black carry bag, and an entrenching shovel.

There was no moon out that night, and he thought it was just plain creepy as he made his way to the camp. He had an idea of how it was laid out from an aerial view he had studied of the camp. He parked his car in the woods about a half-mile away, where it couldn't be seen from the narrow dirt road. He wore black clothing and had the bag on his back as he went to the camp's rear side, where the training occurred. He felt like he was an alone soldier back in Vietnam when he was dropped off in the middle of the woods. He wondered if anyone cared about the mission; he was on to stop the terrorists. Did the Americans think he was just another nut case taking the law into his own hands? Regardless, he had made a promise to Michael, and he would try his best to fulfill that promise, even if it meant dying in the process.

Doug was bent over and moving slowly toward his intended target planting area. He believed this was the same type of land where Michael had trained at Fort Bragg, South Carolina. He found a spot that looked like it was where the terrorist trained in hand-to-hand combat on a concrete slab. There was a six to eight-foot trail the terrorist used to get to their training area. He placed two of his I.E.D. s in that location and two blocks of C-4. Once in place, he wired the I.E.D. s to the C-4, and they were ready to go. There would be a massive explosion when they went off, and hopefully, a lot of terrorists would die. He buried them approximately 20 feet apart and connected them with wire so that when one blew up, the other would blow up. The pressure release plate would trigger them like the ones used in Afghanistan. When a person steps on it, the bomb is set, and when he steps off, it explodes. He camouflaged the area of the I.E.D.s and wire lightly with dirt and leaves from the surrounding area so that everything looked natural.

After these two targets were set, Doug went to the firing range area and set the other two I.E.D. s and C-4 up so they would be ready exactly like he had done at the hand-to-hand combat area. He made sure the bombs were all set with the pressure plates before he left. He grabbed his entrenching shovel and black bag and left quietly as he had come into the camp.

He returned to his car and drove the half-hour drive back to his campsite in Nashville. Once he was back at the motor home, he checked his car's back, so it didn't look like anything was out of place. Satisfied that everything was okay, he settled down for some much-needed sleep.

He got up early, packed up his motor home, attached his car, and took off to Virginia. He was already considering his next target at the "Pink House" in Virginia's remote area. He had read some disturbing things about this camp. It wasn't until a few days after he arrived in

Virginia that he heard the news reports that "The American Terrorist" had struck again in Tennessee.

The news reported eight men were killed and four were wounded in a well-planned and deliberate attack on the camp. It said law enforcement agencies had found two I.E.D. Bombs that had not been detonated. Doug wondered which two didn't explode and wondered why. Did he do something wrong, or once the first two went off and killed the eight men, did they not go near the other two? He knew he couldn't second guess himself because he would never know. The news also reported that Muslims all over America were starting to get very angry, and they believed the CIA or the FBI planned these attacks against the Muslim people.

A spokesperson for the FBI came on the news and said, "I can assure you; this is not the work of the CIA or the FBI. We are just as puzzled as the Muslim community as to who is doing these bombings." He said they would thoroughly investigate this to the fullest extent of the law. They would get to the bottom of who was committing these attacks and put a stop to them. When Doug heard that, he rolled his eyes and said, "I hope not. I'm not through killing these terrorists yet."

In some parts of the South, people were starting to speak up, saying, "It is about time the FBI and the CIA got involved and checked out these terrorist camps. We have been trying to tell them something was going on for the past few years."

Others were saying, "We don't care who is doing the bombings on these camps. We applaud them for having the guts to stand up to these terrorists. These camps have kept most of us born here and lived here all our lives afraid to go out at night." He was happy the people were finally starting to rally behind him and voice their fear and dislike for the terrorist camps located so close to their homes. He felt like he was finally getting the American people's attention.

* * *

Chapter 16 - The Pink House, Virginia

Doug wasn't spending much leisure time between his targets in the South. He figured he better hit them hard and fast, and then he could head north to his following targets. He believed by the time law enforcement agencies started doing thorough investigations of the camp. He would be at his next one and blowing it up.

During his next attack, he would stay at an RV park in Lexington, Virginia, about seventy miles from the "Pink House." It was about a two-hour drive to the camp. His target was a forty-acre parcel eleven miles south of Benmatox, Virginia. He loved this part of the United States because the rolling hills were lush, green, and filled with wildlife. When he arrived at the camp, he could see shacks and trailers believed to serve as safe houses for Muslim Islamic terrorists. He had read some terrible things about the "Pink House."

He read that they have a compound like "Islamtown," which contains an underground bunker system that could be used for training and possibly harbor deadly weapons, maybe even radiological and nuclear devices for use in the great Jihad against the Christian and Jewish people.

In the past, the compound leader, his wife, and another Muslim leader were arrested for illegal arms purchases. Over the years, twenty-four members of this compound have been arrested for trafficking illegal weapons, including ammunition for AK-47s. It is believed that the "Beltway Snipers" took refuge in the Pink House compound between their terror attacks. It was reported that members of the Pink House were involved in a giant fraud scheme right here in America to defraud Americans of their money. The compound regularly receives visits from suspicious guests from Egypt, Yemen, Saudi Arabia, and Pakistan. (23)

Doug believed this was one of the worst compounds he had encountered in his quest to blow up his targets. He had to do something to stop or slow them down. After thinking about it, he decided to try to beat the terrorist at their own game. Since they were receiving incoming and outgoing personnel, he would dress up like a Muslim and try to go into the camp and plant a few bombs. He just had to take his time and figure out how to do it.

Once Doug had a plan in place, he drove around Lexington looking for cars to buy, and he found a 2003 Toyota Camry for sale by the owner parked along one of the streets. It was only a few miles from the RV Park where he was staying. He gave the owner the money and a fake name and signed the necessary papers to transfer the title. The owner quickly signed over the title to him.

After he had the car in his possession, he drove around, found a parking area where people left their vehicles all day, sometimes overnight, and rode with other drivers into one of the larger cities. He took off his Muslim dress, put it in the trunk of his newly purchased car, locked it, and walked back to the RV Park. The following day, he returned to where he had left the car, put the Muslim disguise back on, and headed to the "Pink House Compound."

When Doug arrived at the entrance, he spoke to the guard at the gate in Arabic and was told that he was from Kabul, Afghanistan, and needed a place to stay for a day. The guard didn't understand Arabic, so he told him again in English. He told the guard that a Muslim from another mosque said he might be able to stay a few days at the compound while passing through. The guard told him to check in with the people at the first trailer on the right.

He parked his car, went inside the trailer, and repeated the same story he had told the guard. The man in charge asked Doug several questions about his connection to other Muslim organizations. Doug said he was passing through on his way to Islamcity to see his brother and answered all the man's questions. After he was satisfied with Doug's answers, he told him to go and knock on the door of a bit of a shack about two buildings down. He told him to tell them that Hassib said it was okay to stay for a few days. Before he left, he told Hassib that he had a business in town and would have to drive into town the next day if that was alright. Hassib just nodded, ok.

Doug moved his car to the shack and went to the front door. He had his copy of the Qur'an in one hand and a prayer rug in another. When he knocked on the door, someone said to come in Arabic. As he entered the room, he removed his shoes and closed the door. It was one big open room with several six-inch mattresses on the floor with blankets on top of each mattress. A door led to a bathroom in the back of the room. Three men were lying around relaxing, so he asked them which bed to take. One of the men pointed at an empty bed near the bathroom door.

Doug spent that afternoon lying around and making small talk with a few men, but after a while, he told them he wanted to take a walk. While walking around the camp, he found where he wanted to place his next bomb. There was one main building across from where he was staying that looked like a meeting place, and they were having a meeting the following evening. He decided it would be his target. The guards closely watched him and everyone else while he was in the camp.

He spent a restless night trying to sleep, and the following day, he got up early and drove the Camry back to where he had parked his Mercedes. He took off the Muslim attire and put it under the back seat. He returned to the RV Park in his Mercedes and spent time there so other campers would see him. After lunch, he put some of the C-4 and detonators in a grocery bag, put it in his Mercedes, and then drove back to where he had the Camry parked. He transferred the C-4 and detonators from his Mercedes to the Camry trunk. He left his Mercedes parked in the parking area and took the Camry to an isolated place in the woods. He wore gloves and attached the C-4 with detonators to the frame under the car. After all four blocks of the

C-4 firmly attached and out of sight, he dressed up again in his Muslim disguise and drove back to the "Pink House."

As Doug returned to the camp, the guard recognized and waived him. He parked his car as close to the main meeting building as possible. He went back to his shack and started to relax. About an hour or so later, one of the guards came in. He looked around the room, and when he saw Doug, he asked if the Camry parked outside was his car.

As he slowly stood up, his heart immediately went into his throat, and he thought he had been caught.

He sheepishly said, "Yes, it's my car," as he felt the blood rush to his face. "Is everything ok?"

The guard seemed impatient and agitated. He glared as he said, "No, you have to move it now. We are meeting tonight, and we need that parking space."

Doug told him he would move it right away and asked the guard where he wanted him to move it.

The guard said with disgust, "Move it about twenty yards down from where you have it parked now. Just get it out of the way."

Once he delivered his message, the guard quickly turned and went outside. Doug quietly let out a big sigh of relief, promptly put on his shoes, went outside, and moved the car. Going back to the room, he was thinking. I thought they had caught me with the C-4 attached to the vehicle. I thought I was done. What if they would've found it? They probably would've cut my throat at once. That was a narrow escape and an excellent lesson to learn.

Once he was finished with this target, he wouldn't try this approach again. He was too vulnerable in this position. He became very anxious and restless for the rest when he was at the camp. I'm afraid someone might inspect the car and find his bombs.

He felt like he had to get out of there as soon as possible, but he had to wait until later that day when one of the other men left the camp. Doug asked him for a ride into town and told the driver he would pay for the gas if he would give him a lift. The guy was happy to oblige. Doug was relieved to finally be off the compound because he couldn't wait much longer. Once they got into town, he gave the driver ten dollars and thanked him for the ride.

He quickly caught a cab and had the cabbie drop him off down the road from where his Mercedes was parked. It was just about dusk when Doug finally returned to his Mercedes. He made sure his remote detonator was strapped to his chest as he headed back to the compound again.

When he arrived at the compound, he drove past the entrance to see if the meeting was still happening. He parked up the road from the entrance to watch for the meeting to end. As soon as the meeting broke up and a few cars started to leave, Doug figured this was the perfect time to blow up the Camry. Men were standing around talking in the parking area as he drove past the gate and detonated the C-4 bombs with the detonator.

All four C-4 bombs went off almost simultaneously, and there was a massive explosion. Doug kept driving toward town as though he didn't hear or see anything. On his return to the campground and his attack was completed, he thought the plan had been too risky. He knew that if the terrorists had found his bombs attached to the Camry, he would have been killed. He wasn't ready for that; he had more terrorists to kill.

When he arrived in town, he pulled over in a dark area, took off his Muslim disguise, put it, the detonator, and everything else under the back seat, and drove back to the RV Park. The following day, he got up, made breakfast, and walked around his campsite, enjoying the day. After a few hours, he hooked up the Mercedes to the motor home and was heading to his next destination. He was heading to Washington, D.C., to see the Vietnam Memorial.

As he drove along the highway, he turned on the news, and there was a report of a massive explosion at the "Pink House" in Virginia.

The information reported that twenty-one Muslim people were killed and eighteen wounded in the camp. Doug kept both hands on the wheel as he smiled and thought, Thanks for all the southern hospitality, you scumbags. That one was for Michael. For the first time, the news media reported that people in the South and other parts of the United States were carrying signs that said, "Go home, you Muslim Terrorists," "Get out of our country," and "Thank you, American Terrorist." Doug thought it was working; the people were starting to wake up.

There was also a report of a similar bombing at one of the Muslim mosques in Dallas, Texas, but Doug knew it had nothing to do with him. Other people in America appeared to feel like he did and were getting on his bandwagon. He was happy that this might lead law enforcement away from him for a while, but he was also a little worried that the people who had done the bombing in Dallas might have killed many innocent people. He didn't want "The American Terrorist" to get a reputation for killing innocent women and children.

By now, many Muslims all over the United States were outraged. Some of the extremists were starting to show their actual hand. The National Guard had to be called to calm things down in Tennessee between the Muslims and American "Rednecks."

Doug laughed and thought, I sure opened a new can of worms I wanted. Maybe now America will see the terrorist threat is real right here at home. Perhaps we can start bringing our soldiers home from Iraq and Afghanistan? Maybe we can concentrate more on our homeland security and not foreign countries. Deep inside, he knew that wouldn't happen, but at least it could be a nice dream.

* * *

Chapter 17 - Washington D. C.

Doug learned there are fifty-six FBI field offices throughout the United States. In Washington D.C. alone, eight hundred and fifty-eight Federal agents protect the Capital, the White House, and the U.S. Supreme Court from terrorist plots. He read that every day, there are five bomb threats against one of these locations. According to reports, the agents spend every minute following up on the threats and ensuring they eliminate them. (23)

Doug headed to Washington D.C. and made reservations at the Cherry Hill RV Park, just a few miles from the Capital. It was a perfect place to set up his motor home and visit all the things he wanted to see while he was there. He would try to put his war behind him for a few days and be a tourist. After he arrived at the park and set up his campsite, he kicked back and relaxed and had a glass of red wine. That evening, he mapped out the areas of interest he wanted to visit on his first day in the Capital.

Early the next day, he started with the Washington monument. It is 555 1/8' above the National Mall and is a tribute to George Washington. It was dedicated in 1848. Doug took pictures as he lazily strolled along the concrete pathways. His next stop was the Lincoln Memorial, which was dedicated in 1922 to honor our 16th president, Abraham Lincoln. At the Lincoln site, there is also a memorial to Martin Luther King (a key figure in the African American civil rights movement). Doug had no idea how beautiful and large the memorial was until he stood there. He also saw the 19th Thomas Jefferson Memorial, which was dedicated in 1943 but wasn't completed until 1947. The Roosevelt 32' tall Sculpture was a tribute to the Marines who died in combat since the Marine Corps was founded in 1775.

When he went to the Vietnam Memorial, he found it hard to control his emotions. It was dedicated in 1982 and is called the "Wall." It was one of the main reasons he wanted to stop in Washington, D.C. The "Wall" honors American soldiers killed, prisoners of war, and missing in Vietnam action. Their names are listed chronologically on the black granite V-shaped memorial wall. He spent a few hours there and looked up a few friends' names; he knew he had died in Vietnam.

While sitting on one of the benches at the wall, he couldn't help but think of Michael the entire time he was there. He had to wipe the tears away as he stared at the "Wall" with thoughts of Vietnam and Michael flashing through his mind. He wondered how many more American soldiers would die in the struggle against the terrorists in Iraq and Afghanistan before it was over. He also asked what the memorial would look like to honor American soldiers who died in those two countries someday. He knew that people would eventually see Michaels's name on a monument, and the thought of it felt like a dagger piercing his heart.

Once he regained control of his emotions, he walked past and saw the Vietnam Women's Memorial, dedicated in 1993 to honor servicewomen and nurses. He continued to the U.S. Navy Memorial and Naval Heritage Center. There is a seven-foot-tall bronze statue entitled "Lone Soldier" that stands at the entrance to the U.S. Navy Memorial.

Further down the pathway is the Korean War Veterans Memorial, which was dedicated in 1995. It features a polished wall engraved with the faces of soldiers, nurses, chaplains, and even a dog honoring those who served. The memorial's focal point is a bronze sculpture of platoon soldiers inching through a field. He visited the African American Civil War Memorial and the National World War II Memorial.

Doug finished his first day across the Potomac River, visiting the U.S. Marine Corps War Memorial dedicated in 1954 and the Arlington National Cemetery in Arlington, Virginia. It was designated as a military cemetery in 1864. It is home to over 300,000 honored soldiers and distinguished citizens. When Doug returned to his motor home, he had a red wine and sat down to relax and think about his day. He had no idea how emotionally draining that day would be for him.

He spent all day visiting the U.S. Capitol, The White House, The Smithsonian Institute, The Library of Congress, the National Air and Space Museum, the National American History Museum, The Supreme Court, The Arts Building, and the Pentagon. There was so much to see in one day that he could not spend time in each one. By the end of the day, he was exhausted from all the walking. Back at his motor home, he was kicking back and drinking a glass of red wine when he fell onto his bed and called it a day.

The following day, Doug drove the eighty-three-mile drive to Gettysburg, Pennsylvania, and visited Gettysburg's Battle. It was the Civil War's bloodiest battle, with 51,000 casualties. While there, he also visited the 22,000-square-foot museum at the Gettysburg National Military Park. That trip was a full day and filled with a great deal of pride and sadness. When he returned to his motor home, he had been driving in his car for over five hours and was ready for that glass of red wine.

He kept thinking how great it would have been to visit all the places he had been to the past few days with Shirley, Jenifer, and Michael. Even though he had seen places he had always hoped to visit someday, he was crushed that he had seen them alone. It had a lot of empty meaning to him, the way he felt at that moment. As he sat drinking his wine and feeling very alone and sad, he suddenly snapped back to why he was there in the first place. He was still on his mission to kill the terrorists, and soon, he would be back on the road again, searching for his next target.

That evening, Doug started planning his next target. He decided he would hit the terrorist camp at what many believed to be the Muslim terrorist headquarters at "Islamcity." It is near Francock, New York, only one hundred and fifty miles from New York City. It is deep in the woods and very secluded on a one-hundred-acre compound in the Catskill Mountains. It has winding dirt roads that lead in and out of the area and a guard building at the camp entrance. It reportedly has forty Muslim houses, mosques, schools, grocery stores, and firing ranges.

He believed that with all the media attention about the "American Terrorist," law enforcement would be on full alert for any suspicious activity. He thought that maybe even the FBI and the CIA might be watching for suspicious activity on or near the camp. He had to take his time and be more intelligent in his next attack. He didn't want to kill any undercover law enforcement agents, and he didn't want to get caught by any of them.

Doug would take some time and plan his strategy very carefully, but first, he wanted to drive a little out of his way to see the terrorists' damage to the World Trade Center at "ground zero" in Manhattan, New York. When he arrived at the site and saw the space where the "Twin Towers" once stood, he was floored by what he saw. He and Shirley had visited the "Twin Towers" in May 2001, just before the terrorist blew them up. He remembered how enormous they were to see in person.

It was almost unbelievable because all that was left was just ample space. He was convinced that until you could see this with your own eyes, you would never believe that the young Arab terrorist could have caused that much destruction and devastation here in America. He could still see the images of the two crumbled towers in his mind as he stood there. The anger and hurt welled inside his chest as he recalled how he felt the first time he, Shirley, and Michael watched the news of the attacks on television.

While he was there, he wondered if the Empire State building would someday be a target of radical terrorists. It was built in 1931 and is the tallest building in New York since the World Trade Center's destruction.

While in Manhattan, he also wanted to see the Statue of Liberty. He had to blow off some steam, so he walked several blocks to the water, where there were ferry boat tours to Ellis Island after leaving the Twin Tower site. That is where the "Statue of Liberty" is located. It was a two-hour tour, so he bought a pass and rode to the Island with about one hundred others. When the boat arrived at the base of the "Statue of Liberty," he couldn't believe how beautiful and tall it looked in person. He had that warm and fuzzy feeling in the pit of his stomach. He thought about what this monument represented to all the people of America. He wished Shirley, Jennifer, and Michael could have seen it.

Once he was sightseeing for the day, he returned to his RV campground. He stopped at several places and picked up several "pay as you use" phones. When he was learning how to detonate his bombs, he found out how to take a mobile phone apart, attach a wire to the phone, and another wire into a block of C-4. When the phone receives a call or text, the vibration connection sends a charge that detonates the C-4 bomb. What he liked about them was that you could call the number on the phone detonator from anywhere and set off the explosion. He just had to ensure he didn't turn the phones on until he was ready to use them.

Doug remembered reading about a Russian woman terrorist who had a similar bomb. When she received a text from the phone company, it caused the bomb to go off early, blowing her up before killing hundreds of people on a train she had targeted. Luckily for all the innocent people, she was the only one killed.

Doug had a great plan for some of his future targets, so while in Manhattan, he would visit one of the largest Toys-R-Us stores in America in Times Square. The store has a sixty-foot Ferris wheel near the life-sized T-Rex dinosaur and a 4000-square-foot Barbie Dollhouse. He called the store ahead and told the clerk he wanted two remote control battery-powered adult helicopters fully assembled and ready to fly. He purchased the 450 3-channel metal RC helicopters (called the Silver Ghost). Each aircraft operated on its frequency. They are 31" long and can reach one hundred and fifty feet. They have an operating range of eight hundred feet. They can fly for ten to fifteen minutes with a fully charged battery. He also ordered two remote-control battery-operated Carrera cars, which have four-wheel drives and can hit up to twenty-one miles per hour. They are 19 3/4" long, 10 1/4" wide, and 7" high. He had given it a great deal of thought and would use these remote-control cars and helicopters to deliver his bombs in a few of his future attacks.

On several occasions, while Michael was growing up, he and Doug went to the local school grounds on the weekends, flew remote-controlled airplanes and helicopters, and drove remote-controlled cars. Michael loved to spend time doing it, and he would run them until the batteries were out of juice every time they went. They would have spent every weekend doing only remote-control toys if it had been up to him. Doug was always ready to go because it made him feel like a kid again.

Little did he know that all those weekends flying and driving those remote-control toys would someday be part of his strategy to kill his terrorist targets. When he went into the Toy-R-Us store, he wore his ski cap pulled down over his ears with sunglasses, a mustache and goatee, and a hooded sweatshirt to hide his identity. After he had the toys in his motor home, he found his way out of town, pulled over to the side of the road, and hooked each of their charging units to an outlet in the motor home so they would charge while he was driving to his following location.

* * *

Chapter 18 - Attack on "Islamcity" New York

Before the September 11, 2001 attacks, it was reported that a neighbor of "Islamcity" saw men jogging down a dirt road in military boots and uniforms and carrying weapons in the camp known as Islamcity. The members of this camp are believed to be connected to the Jamaat ul-Fugra terrorist organization. Federal investigators have confirmed that the Jamaat ul-Fugra terrorist organization has been responsible for numerous murders and seventeen bombings in the United States. They have been vigorously attempting and succeeding at recruiting soldiers from the United States prison system. According to neighbor reports, some of their members were observed wearing the New York and New Jersey Port Authority uniforms. The "members" are employed in susceptible infrastructure positions.

At one point, a retired employee of New York's JFK Airport confided to an acquaintance his "vision" for a jihad terror attack that, he said, would attack the World Trade Center and the Pentagon seemed small. The plot involved placing bombs in jet fuel lines in the airport, thereby destroying the airport and probably killing thousands.

It is believed that the ul-Fugra terrorist organizations have stepped up their weapons purchasing and have been stockpiling their weapons for years. They have also stepped up their training at the camp. One member of the organization that had been participating in a training exercise at an Islamic Center in New York said, "We are getting ready—the Day of Atonement is close at hand." (23)

It is precisely the kind of garbage that had driven Doug to the point where he felt America should take the offensive and expel the terrorists that claimed to be members of the Jamaat ul-Fugra and all other suspected terrorist organizations from America. As much as he wanted to believe it was possible, he knew we would never drive them out of America. Regardless, he would continue his assault on their training camps until they were exposed to the everyday hard-working American people.

He made reservations at the Catskill Adventure Resort, which has two hundred and forty RV campsites. It was a perfect spot to hide in full view and wasn't far from his next target. He would stay in this campground for at least one week, do surveillance, and once he was comfortable, blow up his target. When he arrived, he set up his campsite, unhooked his car, and started planning. He met some people camping next to him, and they were friendly and didn't ask too many questions.

A few hours later, he jumped in his Mercedes and drove to the Islamcity camp. He was anxious to look at how the roads were laid out and see the camp in person. All the roads in the area were just narrow dirt roads, and the main road forked at the camp where you could go left or right. He decided to take the road to the left and see where it would lead. The road paralleled the camp for about two hundred yards and then made a substantial left circle back in the direction toward his campsite, but not back on the same road. About a mile from the main entrance to the Islamcity, he found a place to hide his car. It was in the trees about fifty yards off the main dirt road. From there, he would sneak back to the perimeter to do his surveillance and attack the camp. Once he knew he had a safe exit, he returned to the camp and observed it as he drove slowly. There was a guard at the gate, and Doug waved to him as he passed by, but there was no response, just a cold, hard stare.

When Doug was satisfied, he had an escape route and knew how the camp was laid out. He drove back to his campsite and went to bed early. He didn't sleep long and was up by four a.m., and it was still dark. He quickly dressed in his camouflaged uniform. He knew it would be a long day because he would have to stay in the same position and observe the camp with his binoculars. When he arrived to park his car, he got out of the car, put on his night-vision goggles, grabbed his binoculars, and headed to the north end of the camp's perimeter.

He slowly crept into the trees and bushes he knew would give him plenty of cover. He spent the entire day observing the activity in the camp. He observed that everyone except the guards and a few stragglers would attend prayer time in a makeshift shack of a mosque at different times. He watched the building where all the people gathered to eat. He couldn't see where they kept their weapons and did their training, but he lay in a prone position all day, trying to find out everything he could about the camp. He made sure he didn't make any sudden movements or sounds. The perimeter guards would see him.

He observed the camp for the next three days until; finally, the men gathered together and went into an old abandoned flat-top building on the third day. When they came out, they were all carrying AK-47 rifles. He watched as they went to a secluded part of their camp, fired their weapons, and set off grenades and some other explosives. When they were finished, they marched back to the building. As they put their weapons away, Doug whispered, I got you, suckers! Soon, you won't be using that building to hide your weapons. He waited until dark and then made his way back to his car.

That evening, while at his campsite, he ensured one of the helicopter batteries was fully charged. He made a wooden platform about eight inches by eight inches to place the cell phone and a block of C-4. He attached it to the helicopter with four five-foot wires hanging from it to carry the bomb to its intended target.

It was still dark when he left very early the following day. He put the helicopter in the car and everything else hidden under the seat. He ensured he had his cell phone as he headed to the compound. Before daylight, he had the helicopter and its cargo ready. He was hiding as the sun's rays peeped through the trees, and he could tell it would be a beautiful bright day as the activity in the compound started to pick up.

He waited until it was prayer time, and almost everyone was in a building praying. He then turned on the cell phone, implanted the detonator wire into the C-4, and put the helicopter in the air. It was hovering above him with its precious cargo about five feet below it. For a split second, he was proud of himself as he pointed the helicopter toward its intended target and took it up about fifty feet off the ground. He watched it as he maneuvered the craft around a few trees and toward the flat-top building. He set it down on the top of the ammunition building within a few minutes. Once it was in place, he shut it down and left it there. He made sure he didn't leave anything behind as he slowly returned to his car.

After throwing everything under the back seat, he pulled onto the dirt road, heading back to his campsite. When he was about a mile down the mountain road, he turned on the mobile phone in his car and called the mobile phone number on the helicopter cargo plate. There was a slight hesitation when he heard the explosion. Several other secondary blasts followed, and he knew he had reached his target. He smiled as he put both hands on the steering wheel and caught the main road to his campsite. It wasn't long before he kicked back, relaxed, and drank red wine. He knew the FBI would be all over Islamcity once they got word of the explosions.

Doug waited a few days, went into town, and had breakfast at a local café. It was all over the news about the enormous explosions at "Islamcity." The announcement reported that the FBI and other law enforcement agencies had found numerous illegal firearms and explosives at the camp after the explosions. They were now investigating different parts of the camp for additional weapons.

Although the Muslims were outraged over the attack, the American citizens protested the suspected training camps, not just the New York ones. It is what Doug had hoped to accomplish with this target. He wanted the American people to be more informed of the camps and their weapons and not allow the Muslim terrorists to hide the weapons they planned to use against us someday. He felt sure that if the terrorists continued unchecked, the next step would be a dirty nuclear bomb, and they would blow up all of Manhattan, some other major city, or even one of our American nuclear power plants.

He didn't kill any terrorists at this site, but his mission was finished in New York. He was going to head to another mosque that was supposed to be a Muslim terrorist cell in Dove Creek, Michigan. It would be his next target, but he would stop in Chicago, Illinois, before heading there. After staying about a week at the campsite, he packed everything up and headed for Chicago.

* * *

Chapter 19 - Chicago, Illinois - The Protestors

Muslims gather at the most prominent Islamic convention in North America just outside of Chicago every year. It's a four-day convention with an estimated two million Muslims from the United States and Canada each year. The attendees include imams, activists, Muslim professionals, and community groups. Doug wouldn't be there at the right time of the year for the convention. It wouldn't be his target because too many women and children attended.

While in Chicago, he wanted to revisit the John Hancock building, where he had taken Shirley in 1975 during a medical convention. The John Hancock building is the fourth largest in the United States, with one hundred stories, and is 1127 feet high. The building is 897,000 square feet, with offices and seven hundred luxury residential condominiums. It also has a seven-hundred-and-fourteen-car parking garage.

Doug wondered if someday the terrorists may try to blow up the building like they had blown up the "Twin Towers." He knew it had to be one of their primary targets. He had read about the terrorist plots foiled to blow up the nearby "Sears Tower" in Chicago. It is similar in size and height to the John Hancock building, except it is one hundred and eight stories and is 1451 feet high. It is currently the tallest building in the United States since the destruction of the "Twin Towers." (1)

On the drive to Chicago, Doug thought about when he and Shirley dined at the famous "Signature Room" on the ninety-fifth floor. During their dinner, they shared their favorite "Fog Cutter" drink. Shirley said it was a drink in a glass, "Resembled a fishbowl, but nicer." They each had a straw to suck up the ten to twelve shots of alcohol. He remembered how drunk they were as they started to leave the restaurant. He could still see Shirley laughing and the building swaying back and forth as they entered the elevator. Neither knew if the drink caused them to walk so unsteadily or if it was the building. All he knew was that they had a great time that night. Because of Shirley's good memories, he wanted to go there again to relive them.

Doug found an RV resort where he would stay on the outskirts of Chicago. Once he was all settled in, he headed downtown. He called and made reservations to eat that evening at the "Signature Room." Later that evening, as he drove closer to the downtown area, he noticed a lot of commotion in the street.

There were about three or four hundred people along the sidewalks on both sides of the street carrying signs and shouting things like, "Out with the Muslim terrorist," "Muslims go home," "Shut down the Terrorist Camps," and a lot of other things. He was delighted to see this group of Americans on the streets and protesting the Muslim terrorists. His plan to expose Muslim terrorists was finally becoming a reality. His message was finally starting to sink into the American people. Even with this much success, he knew that he couldn't stop his mission now because if he did, the entire mood in America would die down very quickly, and everything would soon be forgotten.

When Doug finished dinner at the "Signature Room," he left the John Hancock building and returned to his campsite. On the way back, he became outraged when he saw another group protesting in the streets. What angered him was that a group of Muslim protestors was carrying signs and saying the Jews, along with the CIA and FBI, were responsible for the bombings on their soft compounds.

He parked his car and went closer to hear what the leading protestors were saying. When he was close enough, he listened to the leaders saying that all the attacks on their camps and mosques were a government conspiracy to drive the Muslims out of America. It amused him as he smiled and thought, "I can't believe this! They are partially right, but it wasn't the government's plan to try and drive the radical

Muslim terrorists out of America, and it wasn't a government conspiracy; it was my plan."

Doug stayed and listened long enough to discover who he thought was the group's leader. In his mid-thirties, a young Arabic-looking man was doing most of the loud protesting and speaking about America and the Jewish people. He was dressed in the typical Muslim attire, wearing sandals, and was holding the Qur'an in his left hand as he spoke to the protestors in the street. The more Doug listened to him, the angrier he became. He made up his mind; he would come back the following day and see if the guy was still spouting off his hatred and lies, and maybe he could find a way to kill him.

That night, after he had returned to his campsite and gone to bed, he tossed and turned, trying to get the Muslim protestors out of his mind so that he could sleep. His anger and frustration kept him awake as he wondered how these people could spread their lies about something they knew nothing about.

The next day, he stayed around camp for a few hours and had lunch. He was deep in thought as he wondered about the Muslim protestors and what he would do. He knew he wanted to do something to let the Muslim protestors understand that the "American Terrorist" wasn't going to sit back and let them spread their propaganda to the rest of the world.

That afternoon, he stuck his second vile of Potassium Chloride in his car and headed downtown to visit the Muslim protestors. Before arriving at their location, he stopped in an empty parking lot and wore his Muslim disguise. He drove past them, parked a few blocks away, and returned to join their chants.

He spent the rest of the day just hanging around in the crowd. He kept an eye on his main target, the group's leader. He had the syringe in his robe pocket, waiting to see how to use it. At one point, his target looked like he was taking a break. One of the building owners where the protesting was taking place had agreed to let everyone use the bathroom inside. As his target went to the bathroom, Doug followed him from a safe distance and went into the bathroom with him.

Going inside, Doug went to one of the stalls nearby and asked the Arabic leader if he genuinely believed in what he was telling everyone in the streets. The leader seemed startled and agitated that this older Muslim man had just asked him such an absurd question.

With anger in his voice, he said, "I believe in my heart every word I'm saying is true and that America and the Jews are behind all the attacks on the Muslim camps, mosques, and the Muslim people." Doug agreed with everything he said as another Muslim man entered the bathroom. He knew he couldn't stick the syringe in the leader here, even though he wanted to. He washed his hands and casually left the bathroom behind the leader.

He wanted desperately to shut this guy up somehow. He knew the truth behind all the attacks and didn't want to see this guy using what Doug was doing as propaganda to spread his hatred toward the Jewish people and the Christians. He stuck around and followed the leader when he left the area. He was with two other men, and they got into an older white van and drove away. He knew they would be back to spread more of their hatred the next day, so Doug was going to take his time and come up with another plan to kill him. He left and went back to his campsite to get some rest.

In the late afternoon of the next day, Doug put his pistol, silencer, and syringe in his car and returned to the Muslim protestor location. Before getting there, he wore his Muslim disguise again and walked into the crowd. He spent the afternoon hanging around the protestors and listening to what they had to say. Listening to their anger and hatred strengthened his resolve to finish his mission.

Doug had found the Leader's white van and parked it close to his vehicle. Later in the day, he went to his car and waited out of sight for the leader and the other two protestors. It was about dark when they finally entered the van and drove away. Doug followed them to an apartment in the middle of town. They dropped off one of the protestors, drove another few miles to some older apartments, and parked in one of the stalls. His target and the other protestor went into a dark apartment building. He followed them and watched closely to see which apartment was theirs.

When they went inside, they turned on the lights, and he could see their silhouettes clearly through the curtains as he watched from outside. Many bushes and ground cover surrounded the buildings, so there were plenty of places for him to hide. He watched them for a few minutes to see what they would do next. After being sure they would be there for a while, he returned to his car, drove down the street, and parked around the corner. He returned to the apartment building with his pistol, the silencer attached and hidden under his robe.

The sidewalk and surrounding area were dark as he made his way slowly to the corner of the building. He walked closer and peered through the curtains to ensure no one else was around. It appeared to Doug that the two men were preparing something for dinner. He aimed carefully at his first target, only about twenty feet away. He squeezed off the first round through the glass window, and his target immediately fell to the floor. Just as the other guy went to his aid, Doug shot him, and he went down. This time, the bullet caused the window to shatter, and the loud sound of broken glass hit the concrete below the window.

He quickly turned and started to walk back to his car. Just as he turned around, there was a young teenage boy about ten yards from him, and it looked like he was heading into one of the other apartments. He was standing there with his eyes and mouth wide open. He looked paralyzed for a short moment. Doug could tell from the fear on his face that he wondered if he would be Doug's next victim. Doug pointed his gun at him, and the only thing he said to him was, "run." He didn't have to say it twice as the young man took off running as fast as he could until he disappeared. Doug figured he would call 911 when he got around the corner and was safe from him.

A porch light came on, and a few apartment doors opened as people started looking outside to see what the noise was all about. He thought the place was getting scary as he ran to his car. Once there, he threw his gun in the driver's seat and drove about five blocks away. When he found a secluded area, he removed his Muslim disguise and put the pistol and everything under the back seat.

He had just left the area when he heard a police siren heading in the apartments' direction. He hadn't gotten more than a mile away when a young police officer pulled him over with his flashing lights. He had his gun drawn and aimed at Doug as he told him to get out of his car with his hands in the air. He slowly opened the door and raised his hands as he got out. Doug said, "Man, they finally caught me. I'm screwed now. Try to stay calm."

The police officer slowly walked over with his gun pointed at him.

Doug said, "What's this all about, officer?" The police officer didn't respond at first, but he could tell he wasn't the Muslim man he was searching for as he got closer. He still asked him what he was doing in the area and where he was going. Doug told him that he was returning to his campsite, where he said he was staying in his motor home, and that he had gone to dinner at the John Hancock building but had gotten lost on his way back.

Doug again asked him what was happening. The police officer said, "We got a report that a Muslim man shot someone at the apartments not far from here. The all-points bulletin said the suspect was driving a car that resembled the one you're driving," He shined a flashlight in the front and back seat of Doug's car to see if anything was suspicious.

Satisfied he wasn't the killer they were looking for, he was in a hurry to return to his search for the killer. He asked Doug if he needed directions back to his campsite, and he told the police officer he had figured out where it was and could get back there on his own.

The officer returned to his patrol car and told Doug he could go. He peeled rubber from his patrol car as he sped away. As soon as he left, Doug sat in the front seat of his car and let out a big sigh of relief as he realized how close he had come to being caught.

If I hadn't taken off the Muslim disguise as quickly as I did, I would now be in handcuffs and heading to jail. Then he thought about the shot of Potassium Chloride being under the back seat of his car. It wouldn't have done him any good if he needed it to inject himself. From now on, he would keep it where he could reach it quickly.

As he drove back to his campsite, he thought the young man he had let run away had given the police the information about him and his car. When he first saw the kid, for a split second, he thought about killing him before he let him run away. He couldn't kill an innocent teenage boy. He was relieved to know the police were looking for a Muslim man and not some retired doctor. Even so, he thought it was too close for comfort. Once he was back at his campsite, he was still pleased with himself as he smiled. Those two Muslim terrorist troublemakers won't lead any more protests and spread hatred and lies in America. They got what they deserved.

* * *

Chapter 20 - Michigan

His following targets would be in Dove Creek, Michigan. Of the one hundred thousand residents there, thirty-two thousand are Muslim. The chief of police is also Muslim. According to what Doug read, despite a court order, the police have enforced Islamic Sharia law in Dove Creek for several years.

Doug felt some of the younger Muslims in America might have a different attitude or belief toward these laws, but as long as they are Muslims, they still believe everyone should follow the Sharia laws.

Since September 11, 2001, there have been ten men living in Michigan or with strong Michigan connections who have been arrested in Terrorism - related cases. The government was convinced that the al-Qaeda terrorists were hiding in southeast Michigan (Detroit). Federal investigators have focused much of the government's "Secret War" on terrorists in Metro Detroit neighborhoods. There has been a massive undercover agent infiltration into the Arab and Muslim communities since 9/11/2001. (23) When he blew them up, Doug hoped the agents wouldn't be near his targets.

One man said to be the leader of a radical Sunni Islam group was fatally shot while resisting arrest and exchanging gunfire with Detroit's federal agents. Agents went to a fifty-year-old male warehouse and tried to arrest him for conspiracy to sell stolen goods and illegally possessing and selling firearms. He and ten others were listed in a criminal complaint. He refused to surrender and fired his weapon at the agents. He was killed by the agents returning fire. He was an Imam or prayer leader of a radical group whose primary mission was to establish an Islamic state within the United States. (23)

Doug had to infiltrate one of the groups and find out where his next target would be. There were too many Muslims in Dove Creek to go in and randomly kill everyone in an entire mosque, including innocent women and children. He was after the radical Muslim terrorists and not peaceful Muslims.

He found an RV Park called Greenfield Village in Dove Creek and set up camp there for a few days. After settling in, he checked around to find where the Muslims talked about hatred toward the Christian and Jewish people. After dark, he drove to a secluded area, put on his Muslim disguise, went to a local mosque, and went inside. He began a conversation with a Muslim man who spoke Arabic. He quietly asked him where he could attend a rally for Muslims against the Jews. The man told him that his mosque didn't support that activity. Doug asked him if he knew a mosque he could go to that did. He gave Doug the names of two groups he said were outspoken about the Jews and Christians. One was in a house on the outskirts of Dove Creek on Rail Street. Doug thanked him in Arabic, quickly left the mosque, and headed home.

When he arrived at the house on Rail Street, he saw a few Muslim men gathered in front of the house, and he knew this was the place. He drove past the house and parked a few blocks away. He still wore his Muslim disguise, so he got out of his car and walked back to the house. As he approached the men standing out front, he asked them if they spoke Arabic, and one of the men replied that he did. He asked Doug in Arabic what town he had lived in. Doug told him he was from Kabul and looking for a place here in Dove Creek with fellow Muslims who believed the way he did about the Jews and Americans. He knew if this guy talked horribly about the Jewish and Christian people. It was the group for which he was searching.

The guy immediately went into a full-blown discussion about how America was guilty of backing up the Jews for their acts of crime against Palestine. Doug just nodded his head in agreement with everything he said. It was the kind of guy he needed to eliminate, and now he was standing there talking to him. He would've liked to pull out a pistol, put it to this man's head, and pull the trigger.

Doug kept his composure and finally asked the guy when the next big meeting would be coming up to discuss everyone's anger toward the Jews and the Christians. He told Doug they have their big meeting every Thursday at 7:00 p.m. That was four days away, so Doug asked him if they had any other meetings he could attend someplace else before Thursday. The guy told him about another meeting that was going to take place in Detroit on Tuesday night. He gave Doug the group and street names but wasn't sure of the exact address. Doug thanked him and told him he would see him at the meeting on Thursday as he headed to his car.

He wanted to find out more about this place in Detroit. When Doug arrived, he drove around for a while in the location the man had given him. He finally found the house on a corner in a rundown neighborhood. It was an older two-story house off the ground about three feet. It had four steps that led to a large, covered, dilapidated porch. Doug was worried about leaving his car in this neighborhood for a very long time, fearing it would be stolen or stripped. As he slowly drove by, he was sure this was the place because there was a lot of activity. Several men sat talking as he glanced through the windows and the open front door.

He had a block of C-4 and a few detonators under his back seat. He waited until the middle of the night to see if he would attach it to the house where it would not be seen. He waited down the street, about a quarter of a mile away, to not bring any attention to himself. He kept an eye on the house for a few hours as he waited. There was a lot of activity that night, with men coming and going.

As he sat there watching until around 1:00 am, a very "scruffy-looking" man tapped on his driver's side window. At first, it startled him because he hadn't seen the man come up from behind his car. He was an African American and looked like one of the homeless guys Doug had encountered a few times during his mission. He had not shaved for a few days, and it looked like he had not showered in several days. When he opened his mouth to speak, Doug saw he was missing one of his top front teeth. His hair was in braids, but it looked loose and dirty. He was wearing a dirty gray hooded sweatshirt pulled up partially over his head. Doug rolled the window a few inches to hear what the guy said. He asked Doug what he was doing just parked there. Doug quickly told him he was from Kabul and was looking for his brother Amid Youssef's house but didn't know where to look.

The guy barked, "I don't think he lives around here. I've never heard of him; his name doesn't sound familiar. You better get out of here. It isn't safe around here at night."

Doug thanked him, rolled up his window, and quickly drove away. He decided to leave this area for a few hours, so he went into the central part of town and waited in a parking lot until later that night.

It was around 3:00 a.m. when he went back to the house that was now his target. He drove around the streets several times to see if anyone was walking around or near the home. After he felt comfortable that no one was watching, he drove around to the side of the house with his lights off. He jumped out of his car with a block of C-4 wrapped in duct tape. He ran up to the house and attached it to an exposed board underneath an open part of the house. He ran back to his car and was gone before anyone could know that he had attached a bomb to the home. During their meeting, he was coming back on Tuesday night and blew the house to pieces. Once he was finished, he drove back to the RV Park to get some much-needed sleep.

It was around noon when Doug finally woke up and started his day. He spent the day just thinking about his other target in Dove Creek and figuring out how he would get the bomb on that location. He didn't like exposing himself in a neighborhood during the daylight. There were too many ways to get caught. He decided this would be the perfect place to dress up as a Parker's Pest Control service representative.

That afternoon, he carried the uniform, sprayer, and pesticide from the motor home and put it in his Mercedes trunk. He drove to a shopping center, parked his car, and put on a baseball cap, mustache, goatee, and sunglasses. He walked to an area where he could take a taxi to a car rental company. He rented a white van under his fake name and drove it to his car, where he got everything from the trunk and put it in the van. He flattened out the block of C-4, attached it to his chest, and stuck the detonator in his pocket. What he liked about C-4 is that you could mold it into any form or shape you wanted, and it wouldn't explode unless it were detonated. You could light it with a match or shoot it with a gun to try to make it explode, and it wouldn't. There had to be some detonator spark that set it off.

When he got to the house, a few Muslim men were standing around talking. Doug went up to one of them and told him he was from Parker's pest control and needed to spray the outside of the house for spiders and insects. The guy just gestured okay with a wave toward the house.

He went about slowly spraying around the base of the house. When he got to the back, he made sure no one was watching as he pulled out the C-4 from under his shirt and stuck it in one of the large cracks in the house's wall. He took out the detonator and stuck it into the C-4, and then it was armed. He sprayed around the other side of the house and back to the front, just like the bomb was set. He kept his rented van and parked it in an overnight public parking lot far from his campground.

On Tuesday evening, he ensured he had his remote detonator as he walked to the van. Once inside, he headed for the house in Detroit. It was around 8:00 p.m. when Doug arrived at the house. Many men were already in the meeting, and several were standing outside. Some of them seemed to be guards keeping an eye on the place. He drove past the house and then pushed the button. The house went up with a loud explosion and a ball of flames. As he looked back in his rear-view mirror, he was pleased with the size of the blast. He drove back to his campsite and relaxed for a few days.

On Thursday evening, he drove by next to his target in Dove Creek and ensured the meeting was in full swing as he pushed the button. As he watched it from his rear-view mirror, he was excited to see the house go up in a loud explosion and huge red flames. He had two hands on the wheel and was smiling. The law enforcement agencies won't have to worry about that anymore.

The next day, he wore his disguise again and returned the van to the car rental company. That afternoon he watched the news as it reported that the "American Terrorist" had struck again in two locations in Michigan. One was in Dove Creek, and the other one was in Detroit.

The news report said that Detroit and Dove Creek's houses had long been suspected of terrorist activity and were under FBI watch. It also reported that eleven men were killed in Detroit and several wounded. Nine men were killed in Dove Creek, and six were wounded. It wasn't the number he expected, but he worked on his mission and kept his promise to Michael and the radical Muslim terrorist organizations.

* * *

Chapter 21 - The Mosque Leader

Doug decided to stay in Dove Creek for a few more days to visit some mosques and meet the Muslim people since so many lived there. He wanted to see how they felt about America and how they lived and believed. What he found during his stay surprised him because most of the Muslim people in Dove Creek appeared peaceful and loving, not bent on destroying Israel or America like the radical Muslim terrorist he was after. He found that Muslim organizations from Dove Creek denounced the attacks on America on 9/11/2001.

One of them was the Islamic Supreme Council of America. They seemed to be a peaceful and genuinely moderate Muslim American organization, and they were not the kind he was after for Doug.

While in Michigan, he learned that a meeting had recently occurred at West Chester University in West Chester, Pennsylvania. The meeting was titled "Islam in America, Intercultural differences." One of the keynote speakers at the University was what many consider the "Most Important Iman" in America for Hezbollah and a supporter of an Iranian imam. He is the head of the Islamic Center in Dove Creek, Michigan. His name is Anwar Zalawinni, and he is the leader of one of the largest mosques in Dove Creek, Michigan. Doug found out he hosted a radical Muslim speaker at his mosque in 1998. The revolutionary speaker delivered a long hate-filled rant against "Jews and Christians." He called Jewish Americans "forces of evil" with a "Satanic mentality." Zalawinni and his congregants gave the radical speaker a standing ovation when he was finished.

When Doug realized this mosque, the leader was also a radical Muslim with strong ties to foreign terrorist organizations. He was angry and knew he would find a way to kill him. Doug thought if he were a good guy, he wouldn't have ties with these radical terrorist organizations. He was angry that Zalawinni was spreading his hatred and propaganda in his mosque to all his members.

He was so angry that he stayed awake most of the night, pacing and thinking about how Zalawinni would be a perfect target for him to kill. He was an older man in his early seventies with gray hair and a gray beard and mustache. He carried himself like a man with a lot of self-worth and pride. The members of his mosque seemed to idolize him for his beliefs and teachings. With this target, Doug had too many women and children that would die if he blew up the mosque. He had to come up with another plan.

He visited the mosque to learn more about Zalawinni's daily routine. He was just the kind of person Doug didn't want in America, spreading his hatred of the Christians and the Jewish people. He wondered how many other hate-filled meetings Zalawinni had held at his mosques, just like the one in 1998.

Doug stayed several more days in Michigan, watching Zalawinni's every move. He followed his car from the mosque to his home every day for five days until he was sure Zalawinni would be where he wanted him when he decided to kill him.

He also watched Zalawinni's neighborhood and found a house about three blocks down the street that looked like the owners might be on vacation. A light was left on in the front, and newspapers had been stacking up for a few days, so Doug knew the owners were probably gone.

While stalking Zalawinni, he kept an eye on the empty house to see if anyone returned. No one had come or gone from home since he had been watching it for five days. There was an alley in the house's back to park his car and make a quick getaway.

One evening after dark, he crept close to the empty house and looked around. Checking the windows and doors, he found everything was locked, so he broke a window in the back door, slowly opened it, went inside, and shut it behind him. After he felt comfortable in the house, he went to the front window and studied his target route.

Watching Zalawinni for five days, he knew he would leave his house about the same morning and head to the mosque. He always drove in the same direction as the empty house. After all his planning, he was satisfied with where and how he would kill Zalawinni.

The night before he was going to kill him, he went back to his camp, cleaned his rifle, and put it back under the back seat of his car along with the bullets he was going to use. He also put the pistol with the silencer in the car as well.

The following morning before daylight, Doug put on the disguise of his hat, mustache, goatee, and black clothes and drove to the spot where he would park his car in the alley. He put the gun and the bullet clip in the black carry bag over his shoulder. He grabbed his pistol and stuck it in his belt. He then went to the empty house and silently slipped inside. He turned no lights on as he opened a living room window covered with a screen. He took up his firing position on his knees and used the window seal as rifle support. He made sure a bullet was in the chamber and the clip was in place. He sat there in silence and waited for his target to drive by.

Like clockwork, Zalawinni started backing out of his driveway and slowly headed in Doug's direction. As soon as he saw him running in his direction, Doug quickly aimed and had him in his sites with the crosshairs on his head. When he drove a little closer, Doug slowly squeezed the trigger and watched in the scope as the bullet went through the car window, struck its target in the head, and parts of his head exploded like a watermelon. He was thinking gotcha! Your evil and hate-spreading messages are over.

He quickly gathered his things, put them in the bag, and put them over his shoulder. He ensured he wiped the doorknobs clean on both sides, even though he had worn surgical gloves during the attack. He was almost in his car when he saw a large Caucasian man approaching him from the corner of his eye. Doug could tell he was big and angry.

As the man tried to grab him by the arm, he said, "Hey, what are you doing stealing stuff from my neighbor? Give me that bag."

Doug didn't say anything to him; he quickly turned toward the man, pulled out his pistol, and shot him in the head. Then he realized the man must have been watching his car and thought he was a burglar when he saw the bag over his shoulder. He looked around quickly to see if anyone else was watching him in the alley, but he didn't see anyone. He threw his bag in the front seat and sped away.

As he drove away, he thought about the man he had just killed and felt the big slob should have stayed out of my business. It was a case of the wrong place and time for that poor fool. He drove several blocks, took off his disguise, and threw everything under the back seat of his car. By killing Zalawinni, he felt he had gotten rid of access to evil in America. He was happy that this man would never spread hatred to his congregation or anyone else.

Doug learned about a "Fish Creek Pass" training camp in Colorado. It was supposed to be another training camp for the radical Muslim terrorists, but he couldn't confirm that it did exist. There was still snow in the area this time of the year, which would've made things a little more difficult for him to reach his target. He decided he would forego that target for now. He knew he had plenty of other targets to take out.

Doug thought there were many individual targets in Pennsylvania, but he wanted to hit the critical terrorist training camps instead of mosques. Now that he had learned more about the radical Muslim training camps from his observations and experiences, he felt they were his best targets. He wanted to focus on the camps because he thought he could kill more of the actual radical terrorists where they were training.

The people in America saw these radical Muslim camps' actual goals, and protests were going on all over America. The American people were increasingly speaking out about the terrorist camps. They wanted the Muslim terrorists out of America, and Doug felt like the snowball effect was starting to occur in America. Several violent clashes were reported between the Christians and the "peaceful and loving" Muslims in America. Doug felt that if we had to fight the terrorist extremists in America, it would be better to do it now than wait until they have infiltrated America to the point of no return.

The Michigan targets were an emotional experience for Doug; he needed a few days to rest and plan his next target. One thing he wanted to see since he wasn't that far away was the Mount Rushmore National Memorial. He was going to South Dakota for a few days and visited the Memorial. He figured he could blend in with the three million visitors that go there each year.

South Dakota was also known for its "Black Hills Gold." Doug had once purchased a ring and matching earrings for Shirley when they were younger, made of black hills gold from South Dakota. It was silver with gold leaves, and he thought the combination looked beautiful.

* * *

Chapter 22 - Ohio

Doug's next target was a suspected terrorist training camp called "Hickory Wood" in Bolster, Ohio, about fifty miles south of Columbus. He would stay at the Lakeview RV Park in Columbus, Ohio. There was talk of a lot of terrorist activity in Ohio, so Doug wanted to check things out for himself.

In 2003, an Islamic terrorist from Columbus, Ohio, was accused and arrested for aiding al-Qaeda and attempting to destroy the

Brooklyn Bridge. He was sentenced to twenty years in prison. In 2006, three terrorists from Toledo, Ohio, were arrested and charged for allegedly planning to build bombs for use by the terrorists in Iraq. One was sentenced to twenty years and received thirteen and eight years in prison.

In 2008, a couple in Toledo, Ohio, was convicted of trying to send $20,000,000 to a terrorist organization in a vehicle they were attempting to ship overseas. Doug was happy when he read that a retired United States Special Forces soldier helped the FBI uncover a "wannabe" training camp in Ohio. Three terrorists had contacted the soldier to help coordinate "Jihad training exercises." What the terrorist didn't know was that the retired soldier was working with investigators all along. The three men raised money for the operations, considered setting up a front charity organization, and used an indoor shooting range for target practice. They were all found guilty and received prison time. (19)

Once Doug was settled in his campsite, he drove to a remote area and put on his disguise: a cap, mustache, goatee, and sunglasses. He then went downtown and walked around to see what information he could find about the training camp at "Hickory Wood." He was told it was about an hour's drive from Columbus and in a remote area of the woods. He knew about the terrorist training camps because they consistently tried to set them up in the most remote areas they could find. They wanted to be away from neighbors and road traffic, and this camp was no different. They try to stay very lowkey until their time is needed to perform their act of terror.

He went back to his campground and just relaxed that evening. The following day, he went back into town. He changed into his Muslim disguise and left his car at a shopping center. He walked downtown until he found an inexpensive but reliable car for a few thousand dollars for sale by the owner. He gave the owner the cash and a fake name and told the owner he would go to the local Department of Motor Vehicles in a few days and change the title to his name. Of course, he knew that was never going to happen.

He filled the car with gas and headed to "Hickory Wood." When he arrived at the camp, there wasn't a guard at the gate, so he cautiously drove into the compound. Not long before, he was stopped by a large muscular guard carrying an AK-47. He asked Doug what he was doing on the compound.

Doug said, "I was looking for a dear brother of mine and was told he might be here."

The guard asked him what his brother's name was, and before Doug could answer his question, he began to ask him other questions to see if his brother was a Muslim and where he was from.

Doug used a similar name to what he had used at one of the other camps as he said, "His name is Amid Youssef."

The guard said in a deep voice, "He isn't in this camp because I've never heard of him."

Doug didn't want to agitate this guard more than he was already, so he said, "Okay, thanks for your help."

The guard seemed very suspicious of him and told Doug to pop his trunk and get out of his car so that he could search it. The guard took his time and looked over the car very thoroughly. He even checked under the seats and in the glove compartment. Doug was happy he hadn't brought his Mercedes with him.

After the guard was satisfied he was not a threat to the camp, he relaxed a bit, and his attitude toward Doug changed. He asked him what his brother looked like, and Doug laughed as he said, "He looks a lot like me but much, much older." The guard chuckled, and Doug knew everything was okay with him from then on.

He asked him if there was a place he could turn around before he headed out of the camp, and the guard said, "Go up to the building ahead and make a U-turn. I will signal the rest of the guards that it's ok." Doug couldn't see the rest of the guards he was talking about, but he thanked him in Arabic. He slowly drove to the building the guard had pointed to, and as he turned his car around, he memorized every building location he could see.

The camp had about ten mobile homes and a couple of more significant older buildings. Behind the mobile homes and buildings was an area where all the trees had been removed. Doug assumed this must be the place where they did their training exercises. He saw trouble attacking this camp because there was only one dirt road into the camp, about seven miles from the main paved road. There was nowhere to hide or escape without getting caught on his way out.

As he drove out, he used his watch and timed how long it took him to go from the camp to the main road. It took him precisely twelve minutes because of the slow and winding dirt road. Once on the main road, he found a place to hide in the trees. He could observe the vehicles that came out of the camp.

After watching for a few hours, Doug followed one of the vehicles coming out of the camp from a distance as it went into town and parked at the local grocery store. He followed it for a few hours until they finally returned to the dirt road entrance. He soon came up with his plan to take out his next target. He returned to the RV Park, still dressed as a Muslim, and told the manager he stayed with a friend in one of the camping sites and paid him to park his newly acquired vehicle for five days. He waited until dark, removed his Muslim disguise, and stuck it in the car trunk.

For the next three days, he drove the car out to the dirt road leading to the camp and observed all the vehicles as they came and went. Each day, he took a sack lunch, water bottles, and reading materials. A white van seemed to be the primary vehicle used the most in the camp. Usually, there were three or four men in it each time it came out of the camp. Doug thought this would be a good target for him. Each day, he followed the same procedure once he returned to the town, parking in the visitor parking area and waiting until dark to take off his disguise.

The night before his attack, he returned to the RV Park, put on surgical gloves, took a block of C-4, and rolled it up in a local newspaper. He attached one of the "pay as you use" phones and the detonator wire to the C-4. Once he had everything in place, he wrapped duct tape around a couple of times at both ends so the bomb and phone were secure. He took two more pieces of duct tape and wrapped it halfway around at each end, leaving enough of it to attach the bomb to the van he had been watching.

The next day, Doug put on his Muslim disguise, took his C-4 bomb, placed it under his front seat, and headed to his observation point again. He took another "pay as use" phone with him. He waited, but to his disappointment, the van didn't come out of the camp that day. That was just a wasted day, but he had now gotten used to waiting and taking his time. He had to come back the next day and wait again.

Finally, the van came out of the camp with four men. He followed it into the town of Columbus. After stopping at a local grocery store, two men got out and went inside, and the others stayed in the car. When the two men were finished shopping, they drove to an older part of town and parked in front of an old house in the middle of the block surrounded by other homes. All four men got out of the van and went into the house.

After they went inside, Doug drove past the house, and he could see other men greet them, and it looked like they were having a meeting. It was the middle of the day, and a few people were walking around the neighborhood. He wondered how to attach his bomb to the van with all this activity. He figured he only needed five seconds to attach the bomb to the van since everything was ready. He had to wrap the two loose duct tape pieces partially wrapped around the bomb to one of the wheel bars under the van. The bar was exposed and easy to reach, but he couldn't let anyone see him do it. He had to create some diversion to take the attention off him and the van.

Doug drove down the street and got the address of a house about two blocks away. He called the local fire department and told them a place was on fire at that address. He drove about a block from the van, got out, and started walking toward it. He had turned on the phone that was attached to the bomb. He then put the bomb under his Muslim robe. It wasn't long, and a few fire trucks glared down the street past him.

People came out of their houses to check out what was going on. Some people were running in the street and following the fire truck. Doug walked along the road near the side of the van as if looking at what was going on. When he got close enough to the van, he quickly bent down as if checking one of the tires and attached the bomb to the wheelbar. Doug then turned around and hurried back to his car. He didn't know if anyone saw what he had done, but he wasn't taking any chances as he jumped into the car and left. They did their everyday business when everyone realized it was a false alarm.

Doug drove back to his hiding place across from the dirt road entrance to the camp and waited for the van to return. After about two hours, the van pulled into the dirt road and headed toward the camp. He timed the van from where it left the main road to what he thought would be the camp. He waited fifteen minutes to ensure they had no unexpected stops along the way. Then, he turned his phone on and called the phone attached to the bomb. He heard the explosion in the distance and knew he had gotten another target. He drove to a shopping center near his campsite, wiped the car clean, made sure there was nothing left in it, and left it there. He removed his Muslim disguise, put it in a shopping bag, and returned to his campsite.

The next day, the news that the "American Terrorist" had struck again on a camp near Columbus, Ohio, and six men and one woman were killed and two wounded. Doug was disappointed that his bomb didn't get a few more from the camp, but at least he got seven, which would get the attention he wanted.

According to news reports, the explosion had gotten law enforcement attention, and he figured that would be good enough. He knew law enforcement would be doing a full investigation into the camp since it was one the "American Terrorist" had targeted. Law enforcement had already figured out by now that the only targets the "American Terrorist" was hitting were the ones where there was suspected terrorist activity.

Doug read in the local paper that because of all the protests that were going on in the United States, "The government decided to do some Martial Law Drills conducted by the FBI and Department of Homeland Security (DHS), in Indianapolis. It was a coordinated effort by the Mayor of the town and the military in twenty-six areas, and it involved two thousand three hundred Marines. It lasted two weeks, and they put the Marines in a police role to do civilian law enforcement. It seemed to be a major objective of the exercise."

According to the official story, the Marines were there for pre-deployment training in a realistic urban environment. The commanding officer said, "Our aim in Indianapolis is to expose our Marines to realistic scenarios and stresses posed by operating in an actual urban community." The government wanted to understand how everything was conducted and how people would react to this taking over. (7)

Doug knew the government was getting ready if they had to use the Marines to impose martial law in cities and towns across America if they had to stop rioting or aggression caused by all the protestors and Muslim terrorists. He was happy to see the government step in and do this type of training. He felt like it was at least a step in the right direction. He knew it would be needed if the Muslims and Christians ended up in numerous clashes in cities throughout America.

Doug hoped the American people would start protesting the war in Afghanistan to bring our American troops home as they had done during the Vietnam War. He thought, why should we be fighting terrorism in Afghanistan and other countries when we have our hands full right here in America? He hoped America would see the ongoing threat at home regarding the terrorist organizations and put pressure on the President of Congress. The rest of the government to stop the killing and maiming of our young men in those countries.

After being on the road for a few months and blowing up his targets, Doug wondered if his vengeance acts were affecting the Muslim terrorist organizations. He also wondered if his efforts to inform the American people of the terrorist hiding places would impact the Government fighting against terrorism. Regardless, he wasn't going to stop his mission. He still had a lot more targets he was going to hit.

* * *

Chapter 23- Georgia

Doug's next target was the suspected "Fish Camp" terrorist training camp at Cummings, Georgia. It's a one-hour and twenty-minute drive from the large city of Atlanta. Neighbors living next to "Fish Camp" claimed they had heard gunfire and small explosions coming inside the camp. One neighbor who was looking for his lost dog stumbled onto the area of the camp by mistake. He was followed for several miles by someone from the camp before they turned around and went back when he left. They have also heard recorded calls to prayer and other strange sounds from the camp. The Islamic people have prayer time five times a day and practice it faithfully.

The population of the beautiful little town of Cummings is only around 6,575. The people were so friendly that Doug thought for a fleeting moment that Georgia and a little town like this one were where he would like to settle down again someday if he were alive after his mission was completed. He would stay at the Jones RV Park, north of Atlanta and a little closer to Cummings and his target.

He thought when he got to Cummings. He would fish along the Hudson River and check out his next target. He would stop at one of the large sporting goods stores to pick up fishing gear, a fishing license, and a rubber raft with a battery pump. He was almost to his destination after a few days of traveling, seeing the sites, and taking pictures. He had to make a scary and unscheduled stop before Doug got to the Jones RV Park in Atlanta.

While traveling on the interstate, he was waived over by a passing motorist. Doug rolled down his window to hear what the driver was saying. He told Doug he had a flat on his Mercedes and motioned toward his car. Doug thanked him and pulled off to the side of the road to see the damage. One of the rear tires on the Mercedes was pretty chewed up, and it was just riding on the rim. He needed to unhook the car from the motor home and change the tire.

Right in the middle of changing the tire, a state trooper pulled behind him. Doug thought, "Oh great. What does he want?" He quickly jumped out of his car, put on his little Canadian Mounty look-alike hat, and headed in Doug's direction.

Doug jumped up and glanced inside his trunk to ensure everything was hidden before the trooper approached his car. When the trooper got close to him, he asked him if he needed any help.

Doug looked at him, laughed, and said, "No, I think I have it under control. I've changed a lot of these in my day."

The trooper laughed, saying, "I bet you have, but probably never one while towing it behind a motor home."

Doug laughed and said, "Yea, this is a first."

He couldn't believe how young this guy looked. He looked like he may have just gotten out of college or some military school. He was in excellent shape, which reminded him of how Michael looked the last time he saw him.

As the trooper stood there, it seemed to Doug that he just wanted to have someone to talk to for a few minutes. He didn't think the trooper wanted to dirty his freshly starched slacks. He asked Doug if he enjoyed his travels across the United States as he looked at the California License plates. Doug told him about the stops at the Grand Canyon, Oklahoma, Nashville, and the Grand Old Opry to take his mind off the California plates.

After about twenty minutes, he had the tire changed, and the trooper finally said he had to get back to work. Doug thanked him for stopping and for offering to help. He was glad the trooper was friendly and not just looking for an excuse to check the inside of the motor home. Once the trooper was gone, he headed into Atlanta and thought how lucky he was that the trooper hadn't gone inside the motor home.

He knew he had a few things lying inside that he didn't want the trooper to see.

The first night he was at his RV camp, he drove into Atlanta to have dinner and attempt to relax. He made reservations earlier to dine at the "Sun Dial Restaurant," seven hundred and twenty-three feet above the city. It has sweeping views from a rotating restaurant at the top of the Westin Peach Tree Plaza. It reminded Doug of the Space Needle in Seattle, Washington. He felt this was just what he needed to relax his mind and body for a little while.

When he arrived at the restaurant, he told the young girl, "This is a beautiful view from up here. I'm glad I chose this restaurant. Is the food as good as the view?"

The host laughed and said, "Even better, but you will find out for yourself," as she ushered him to his table.

After dinner, he sat briefly and sipped a red wine, nursing it as long as possible. He was thinking as he sat there enjoying the view of the city lights. I'm a long way from what I used to call home. I sure miss my old life with Shirley, Jenifer, and Michael. I wish I could have it all back and forget about all this killing.

At that moment, he felt displaced, vulnerable, and lonely. He thought the entire world seemed large from up there, especially compared to when he was out in his little hiding places, doing surveillance and spying on his targets or blowing them up. He felt like maybe he was the only one in the world that cared about what was going on with the radical terrorist outside those windows. For a moment, he wondered if his actions made sense to anyone but him.

He felt sorry for himself again and longed to have Michael by his side. He was thinking. I wish you were here, Michael. I sure miss you. With tears, he lifted his glass and said, "This is a salute to you, Michael. I love you."

The following day, he was composed and focused once again and spent some time getting all his fishing gear and raft ready to go. As he left the campground, he put on his ski cap, mustache, goatee, and sunglasses and headed for Cummings to pay an unsuspecting visit to "Fish Camp." When he got to Cummings, he went into one of the little local home-cooking restaurants called the "Dew Drop-In" and ordered a hot turkey sandwich.

While waiting for his lunch, one of the waitresses seemed like she liked talking and came over to his table. She reminded him of a typical pretty southern girl with beautiful, long dark hair and dark eyes. She was wearing an apron around her skirt and top. She had a bubbly personality and talked to each customer in the restaurant for several minutes.

When she came to his table, she made him feel at home, so he asked, "This may be a silly question, but do you know a good place to fish along the Hudson River?"

She smiled, hesitated momentarily, tipped her head to one side, and said, "Are you in a boat or just fishing from shore?"

Doug replied, "I have a rubber raft with a couple of oars, but do you think the water is too fast right now?

She thought briefly and said, "Not this time of year. The water is moving fairly slow, so you should be okay."

He thanked her for the information and said, "I heard there's an Islamic camp somewhere along the river they call "Fish Camp," do you think I will have a problem with the people from the camp if I get near their property?"

She wrinkled up her nose and smiled, saying, "Not if you stay on the right side of the river. Just ensure you stay along the bank because they don't like trespassers if you accidentally get on their camp."

He nodded as if he understood and asked, "How will I know when I am on or near their property?

She replied, "Oh, you will know. You will see the signs all along the river that says no trespassing."

He again thanked her and said, "I have another question for you, and then I'll stop bothering you.

Where is the best place to put a raft in the river?

She said, "The camp is on the other side of the riverbank, so if you take this little dirt road right out here, " she pointed at one of the dirt roads leading out of town. Going about eight miles, you will see a turn-out where the river makes an L-shaped bend. That's where everyone swims in the summertime because it's deep."

Because she was so friendly and helpful, he asked her one last question, "Do you know where I can get some bait?"

She said, "There is a little grocery store around the corner, and they can sell you some worms or whatever you want."

Doug thanked her for all her help, and as he left the restaurant, he gave her a nice big tip.

He drove to the spot she'd recommended but made sure he took his time getting there. He was checking things out along the dirt road for a hiding place for his car. He needed an escape route to get out of there in a hurry. Doug found an excellent place to park his car in the thick brush that wouldn't be seen from the road. He blew the raft up, put the fishing gear in it, and walked it down to the river. He carefully got in the raft, and away he went down the slow-moving river. He rigged up his pole, put a worm on the hook, and started fishing as he drifted down the river. He caught some good-sized trout but turned them loose while looking for the terrorist camp. He would've liked to take them back to his campsite and have them for dinner, but he didn't want to be sidetracked with cleaning fish while on his mission.

When he finally drifted close to "Fish Camp," he could see their signs along the east side of the river, just like the waitress had said. After passing a few road signs, he jumped out of the raft and pulled it to shore. He walked along the river's edge, casting his line and waiting to see if anyone would show up to make him leave.

After several minutes of not seeing anyone, he crawled to the top of the riverbank to observe the camp. The camp was much like his other targets, with mobile homes and some loosely put-together shacks. Some people were milling around, and others seemed to be in a hurry to get to where they were going. He watched from a crouched position, with his binoculars, for about thirty minutes.

The area was thick with brush and trees, but the camp had been cleared around the camp's buildings and other parts. He couldn't tell what the buildings were used for, but one building was getting more traffic than the others. He didn't see any children and only a few women walking around. Since he couldn't observe the entire camp from any other position, he felt he was pressing his luck, staying there much longer. From what he could tell during his observation of the camp, the building with all the traffic would be his best target.

He pulled his raft back into the water, jumped in, and drifted down the river. He paddled to the shore about a half-mile past the camp, pulled the raft out of the river, and deflated it. He then hid the raft in some heavy brush along the road and hiked back the few miles to his car. Once in his car, he returned to where he had hidden the raft, stopped, opened the trunk, and threw the raft and fishing gear inside. He had to remember this spot because he would make the same trip again in a few days.

Doug drove back to town and took the road on the other side of the river, which looked like it might also go in the camp's direction. After driving for several miles, he found the camp entrance and drove to the guardhouse. He wanted to see how things looked from that side of the camp. He looked things over as he waved to the guard and slowly turned around.

It rained all the next day, so Doug spent the day charging the battery to the Silver Ghost helicopter and getting the detonator phone ready for the aircraft and one for the I.E.D. he was going to plant near the guardhouse. He enjoyed listening to the rain beating down on the motor home. It reminded him of when he was a kid, and they had this building attached to the barn, which had a tin roof. He loved to sit under it during a rainstorm and listen to the rain beat down on that roof. Sometimes, during a rainstorm, he would sit under it for hours and let his mind zone out.

It was dark and gloomy as it rained for two more days. Doug was anxious about hitting his target and didn't want to wait much longer. In the middle of the night, he decided to make his move. He dressed in black and headed for the spot along the river he had picked out earlier. He put the helicopter and the phone detonator in the trunk. He had wires and a frame attached to it, just like he had done at "Islamcity." He also took an I.E.D., phone detonator, and entrenching shovel and put them in his black bag in the trunk. When he got to the river, he aired up the raft, put everything in it, and hid it in some brush along the river. He drove his car to its hiding spot down the dirt road and returned to where he had hidden his raft in the thick trees.

It was utterly dark, and the rain clouds were black as they poured down. Even though he had on a black raincoat, he was soaked as his raft made its way to the "No trespassing" signs in the river. He pulled the raft over to the side of the embankment. He hid the helicopter and the raft under the brush and trees. When he crawled to the top of the embankment, he could see a little light shining in the distance where the guard post was located.

He took the bag with everything in it and methodically walked along the tree line to the light. He didn't see the guard when he was within forty yards of the little building, so he believed he stayed in the guard building and out of the rain. He figured the guard was looking and listening more for a vehicle's lights and sound than someone on foot. When he got closer, he lowly crawled within a few yards of the guardhouse. He swiftly dug a hole in the soft, wet ground with the entrenching shovel, quickly removed the I.E.D. from the bag, and placed it in the spot. He attached the phone to the I.E.D. and turned it on. He covered the hole and low crawled back to where he had hidden again in the trees.

He slowly reached the raft, got under it for cover, and waited for morning. He was shaking from head to toe from being so wet and cold. He sat there thinking he couldn't ever remember being that cold in a long time. He tried to take his mind off the cold, but nothing helped. The sun never rose when it got close to morning, but the rain slowed down a bit.

He couldn't take the cold much longer, so around 6:00 am, he went up the hill with the armed helicopter and the extra phone in his bag and turned on the phones. He phoned the number that was attached to the I.E.D. Near the guard entrance. He heard the explosion from the front gate and people shouting and running. He turned on the helicopter and put it in the air. He maneuvered it around a few trees and set it down next to the building he had planned to blow up. He dialed the number on the helicopter phone, and it exploded. He didn't stick around to see the damage as he immediately pulled the raft down to the water and jumped in with the black bag. He quickly put the remote control in the black bag, pushed it off the bank, and started floating.

As he floated down the river, he felt utterly vulnerable the half-mile to his disembarking point. That was one time he wished the water would have moved faster. Once he was out of the water, he put several holes in the raft and sank it to the bottom of the river. He wasn't worried about prints because he wore surgical gloves for everything he did with the raft.

He was soaking wet and freezing when he made it to the car. He quickly jumped in, started the engine, and turned the heat up as high as possible to warm up. He put the black bag under the back seat, and soon he was on the dirt road heading out of there and back to his campsite. He was exhausted when he returned and could finally shower and wear warm clothes. He spent the rest of that day having a few cups of hot chocolate and relaxing before falling asleep early that evening.

The next day, he listened to the news reports and heard that he had killed sixteen men, three women, and two young children. When Doug heard about the children, he had to turn the news off because he was angry with himself. He never wanted to kill a child. He knew in his heart that he should have studied this target more. His fear of this camp and how it was set up and laid out made him move on it quicker than he would have liked.

He was having a battle within his head, and the tears wouldn't stop flowing because of the children. He thought, "You crazy fool, now you are just like the terrorist you've been trying to kill. Why didn't you take time and make sure there were no children?" He wasn't so concerned about the women because he knew some were just as deadly as the men in their terrorist desires. The little children had nothing to do with their parent's terrorist activities, and he was hurting for the first time since he started his mission to kill the terrorist.

Hours later, he could calm himself down and remember what his Pastor had told him about killing people during an act of war. He now had to rely on his faith to get him through his feelings of guilt. He also remembered what his commanders in Vietnam said when the American soldiers killed women and children. His commander always said, "They are all enemies regarding war. The women and children are just an unfortunate part of the casualties of this war." He tried to accept this explanation, but the children's death still haunted him.

That night, he got down on his knees, put his hands in a praying position, and said, "God, please forgive me for killing the children. I never meant for that to happen. I know the innocent children had nothing to do with their parents' actions. They were just in the wrong place at the wrong time. I am so sorry for what happened to them. Please forgive me, Amen." He knew there would be many repercussions from the Muslims and Christians of America regarding the children, but he could do nothing to change what he had done.

He had everyone's attention, and the news media was everywhere. The protestors from the south were angry about the camps being in their backyards. Some local people were saying to the press, "Thank you, "American Terrorist," for opening the eyes of the rest of the people in America. Maybe the government will now come in and inspect this place for weapons and other propaganda and start getting the terrorists out of America." Some so-called "Rednecks" talked about taking the law into their own hands to eliminate the terrorist camps.

One young man interviewed by a CNN reporter said, "If they want to kill all of us Christians, then I think we, as Americans, should hit them first before they have a chance to hurt or kill our families. We have guns; we should give them one if they want a fight." The reporter asked the young man, "What do you think about the children and women killed at "Fish Camp?" He said, "Well, I feel sorry for the little kids that were killed, but the women knew what they were doing and were part of the terrorist plan to kill Americans, or they wouldn't have been in the camp in the first place. It is just unfortunate the kids were born into this type of family and hatred." He told the reporter, "This is why we should do something now. I have two young boys, and I don't want them to grow up in an America where the terrorists rule our lives."

The reporter interviewed an FBI liaison, Eric Haden, and asked him his thoughts.

He replied, "If the "American Terrorist or Terrorists," we're trying to get our attention, then it worked. We have people working overtime in all the locations they have attacked, and we are trying to anticipate their next target." He said they would find the person or persons responsible for all the attacks and bring them to justice. He said, "They will make a mistake sooner or later; they always do, and we will catch them."

The reporter asked the FBI Liaison, "Do you have any leads on who may be behind the attacks?"

He said, "I believe they have several they are following up on as part of the ongoing investigation."

The reporter thanked him for his time and said, "Good luck," as she signed off.

Doug knew they didn't have anything on him yet, or they would have known he was working alone. He thought, "Do your job, Eric, and find the real terrorist organizations, their camps, and the holes they hide in and end their terrorist activity. Stop looking for a lonely old doctor that wants what's right for his grandson (revenge and justice) from the terrorist organizations."

After watching and listening to the news, he decided to find a target somewhere other than the South. He already had the people in the south all riled up and right where he figured they needed to be. There were still two known training camps in Ingham and Jethro, Georgia, that Doug wanted to hit, but with all the attention from law enforcement, he couldn't take a chance in hitting them because he figured the camps would be on high alert, and maybe just waiting to catch or kill him.

There were also suspected terrorist cells in Orlando, Miami, Ft. Lauderdale, and Boca Raton, Florida. Still, after researching that area, he was sure the FBI and other agencies watched these groups very closely. He knew that neither of these places would be safe for him with the current situation in the south and the surveillance of groups in Florida. He decided to stay on the move to seek a new terrorist target.

* *

Chapter 24 - Texas

Doug would stay at the Four Winds RV Park just outside of Houston. The more he read about the different terrorist attacks or plots that have been foiled in America, the more he wondered if any places in America were genuinely safe from these terrorist organizations. When he read about the terrorist activity in Texas, he wasn't surprised to find they had their fair share of terrorist attacks.

A twenty-year-old Saudi Arabian came to the United States in 2008 and attended Texas Tech University. He was arrested in Lubbock for allegedly targeting the Dallas home of former President George W. Bush and planning to use chemical weapons on other targets in America. Five foreign nationals (French Moroccans) were arrested after a failed attempt to break into the Bexar County Courthouse in San Antonio, Texas.

The FBI has been figuring out why the group traveled extensively to high-level security facilities around the United States. They had maps, computers, and other suspicious documents.

A nineteen-year-old suspected Muslim terrorist was arrested and charged that he intended to bomb a downtown Dallas skyscraper. Still, one of the most publicized incidents at Fort Hood was when a thirty-nine-year-old U.S. Army Major shot and killed thirteen people (twelve soldiers) and wounded twenty-nine (soldiers and civilians) at the U.S. military base. He is an American Muslim of Palestinian descent. (23)

Doug's next target was a large house located in Houston, Texas. He had studied reports indicating the organization members who lived there supported and praised some of the terrorist attacks in America during the past. They held meetings at the house for new and old members.

When Doug woke up the following day in Houston, he stretched out his arms, took a deep breath, and thought, this feels good, as he took in the warm sun and Houston air. He got in his car and headed downtown to the famous Copper Penny Restaurant that made a hearty home-style breakfast. He was seated in front of a hot plate of two eggs with a thick slice of ham, hash browns, biscuits and gravy, and a glass of milk. He thought, "Man, I haven't had a breakfast like this in a long time."

After he left the restaurant, he went to check out his next target. When he found the house, it was in an area with many empty commercial buildings with broken windows. The house was an old commercial flat-top building the Muslims had made into a home. It was located between two other buildings that were connected. It had a twenty-foot concrete walkway from the main sidewalk to the front door. The place wasn't at all what he expected to find.

He returned to his RV campsite and relaxed for the rest of the day. That evening, he put his Muslim disguise in his car, headed to a secluded place, and put it on. He drove to the house and parked down the street. It was about 7:00 p.m., and people were entering the home. To Doug, it looked like they were having a pretty good size meeting. He walked up to one of the men standing near the door entrance to the building and asked him in Arabic if he understood Arabic.

He laughed and said, "Yes, but I prefer English."

Doug asked him if the meeting would be held that talked about the Jews and Christians, and the man said yes.

He asked the man, "Will I be welcomed here?"

He looked at Doug in bewilderment and said, "You are a Muslim, aren't you?"

Doug replied, "Yes, all my life."

The man said, "Then you are welcome here," as they walked inside the house together.

The building's central part was stripped of any wall pictures and was one big open room with folding chairs set up in rows. There was a podium in the front where the speaker stood. Doug noticed fliers on a fold-out table at the back of the room, which looked like the ones he had seen. The man walked over and grabbed two of the fliers, and gave him one. He followed the man to a seat, sat down, and examined the flyer.

It wasn't long before the main speaker, who had been talking to a few other men in the front row, got up and called the meeting to order. They had a Muslim prayer for their first item on the agenda, and then new people who had never been there had to get up and introduce themselves. When it was Doug's turn, he stood up and began to say who he was and where he was from in Arabic.

The meeting started like any other Muslim meeting, with a general talk about the Qur'an and what Allah expected of his people. As the meeting progressed, the speaker's valid message and the forum's people started to come out. The more the speaker spoke insults about the Jewish people, Israel, and America, the more the group became heated and cheered with approval. He just played along with them and joined in. By the time the meeting was over, he was sure several men in the group would have gladly strung him up by his heels and cut his throat if they had known he was a Christian and there to spy on them. He thought they probably would have skinned him alive if they had known he was the "American Terrorist."

As he left the building, he thanked them for allowing him to attend the meeting and asked the man he had been sitting with when the next meeting would be. He told him the next one would be the day after tomorrow, and they had a guest speaker from out of the area who would be there. On the way to his car, he thought, "Yes, this is my target, and I am going to blow them up."

The next day, Doug dressed in a cap, mustache, goatee, and sunglasses after leaving the campground. He went downtown and bought a 2002 Toyota Corolla for sale from the owner. It was a little beat up, but the engine ran well, which mattered to him. He drove to his next target area to determine his best attack plan and escape route. He decided to use one of the remote-control cars he had purchased to see how well it would work. He thought this was ideal because of the flat sidewalk up to the building. He looked around and saw an abandoned building across the street about eighty yards from his target. It was perfect; he had a clear view of the building and could operate the remote-control car from that position.

Before returning to his campsite, he removed his disguise and parked the car in the visitor's campground area. He ensured no one was in the area as he exited the car and walked to his campsite. That night, he spent some time recharging the battery for the remote-controlled vehicle and attaching a C-4 bomb and phone to it. He inserted the detonator wire into the C-4, and it was ready.

Doug was up before daylight, put his Muslim disguise and the remote-control car in the black bag, and went to where he had parked the Toyota in the visitor parking. He put the bag in the trunk, along with the controller and his extra phone. He then drove to the abandoned building and parked a few blocks away down the street. He got the car and phone out of the trunk and made sure no one was watching as he found a place in the abandoned building to hide for the rest of the day.

Men started making their way into the building when the meeting drew near. The one thing Doug didn't count on was a big truck parked in front of the building where he was hiding, completely blocking his view of his target. He knew he wouldn't control his car from where he was positioned, so he had to move to a different location.

He quickly changed his plans, leaving the building, returning everything to his vehicle, and putting them in the passenger side's front seat. He then drove to the same street side as the building, about fifty yards away. The sidewalk was clear to the house, and he had a good view of the sidewalk from where he sat in his car. He would control the vehicle from inside the car to the walkway that led to the house. He waited until all the men were in the building, and the sidewalk was straightforward. He went to the passenger side, got the remote-controlled car out, sat it down on the sidewalk, and turned on the phone. He had it headed toward his target as he got back into his car and started to send it on its mission.

Just as he started to turn the remote-control car on, a kid about twelve years old appeared out of nowhere and was heading right toward the remote-controlled car. The kid skipped along like he didn't care about the world until he saw the vehicle and froze in his tracks. Doug could tell this kid thought he had just found a pot of gold. He looked around and then started to head toward the car slowly. When he got within a few feet of the car, he looked over at Doug, hesitated a minute, grabbed it, and started to run. By then, Doug was already out of the car and chasing after him. He felt lucky when he caught the kid by the collar and told him to stop.

The kid was kicking and wiggling around as he said, "Hey man, I am going to start yelling if you don't let go of me right now, and people will be all over you."

Doug figured what he was saying was probably true, so he let go of the kid and said, "I'm sorry, but that is my car you have in your hands, and it is not a toy."

The kid looked at the car and then looked back at him and said, "Well, it's my car now, and you ain't getting it back."

Doug couldn't believe he was standing there arguing over his car with a bomb attached, and the kid wasn't budging an inch.

He looked into the kid's dark brown eyes and said, "Ok, here's the deal: I need to get that car back, and if you give it back to me, I will give you fifty bucks."

The kid looked at him, hesitated momentarily, and said, "No way, man, make it a hundred bucks, and I'll give it back to you."

He couldn't believe the nerve of this kid. After all he had been through on his missions, a twelve-year-old kid was blackmailing him.

He rolled his eyes and said, "It's a deal," as he pulled out a hundred-dollar bill, held it out to the kid, and told him, "I will give you another fifty bucks if you get out of here and don't come back until tomorrow."

The kid was initially reluctant but must have figured he wouldn't be able to keep the car anyway, so he said, "Ok, it's a deal."

He grabbed the money and sat the car down on the sidewalk as he ran in the opposite direction. Doug was thinking, "Whatever happened to respect for your elders? Michael would never have been that disrespectful to an older person."

He immediately gathered up his precious car, returned to his vehicle, and collected his thoughts for a minute. After he composed himself, he decided to put the car back on the sidewalk and finish the mission. He ensured the phone was on as he started it toward his target. It worked great as it got to the sidewalk leading to the building. He turned the car in an L shape toward the house and slowed it down to a crawl because he couldn't see it once it started toward the house. He wanted it to touch the house gently and not disturb the meeting. He wasn't positive it was against the building, but after a minute or so, he thought it might be in position. He quickly made a U-turn in the road and headed in the opposite direction as he dialed the number on the phone and detonated the bomb. There was a massive explosion, and as he looked back in his rear-view mirror, he could see the flames and debris shooting up about twenty to thirty feet into the dark sky.

On his way back into town, he thought, "That kid almost ruined my whole day and maybe my entire mission. That was too close for comfort once again." He thought the car idea might be too risky to remove his targets. He decided never to use that type of attack again. The next day, he relaxed at the campground and reflected on some of his good memories with Michael, Shirley, and Jenifer. Sitting there, he whispered, "Hey Michael, I got another target for you, so I have them on the run now."

Later that day, the news reported that the "American Terrorist had hit a Muslim gathering place," and twelve men were killed and sixteen injured. Once again, there was protesting from the Muslim community, and the clashes between Muslims and Christians became more frequent and violent.

On Good Morning America, they interviewed the liaison for Homeland Security, a retired FBI agent. He said I'm surprised that the Houston area had been attacked since there weren't supposed to be any suspected terrorist buildings in the area.

Houston's suspected terrorist training camp was supposed to be shut down several years earlier. After it was disclosed, the terrorist organization had weapons and was training in the camp. He said they didn't know about this Muslim meeting house, so "Maybe the American Terrorist" knew something we didn't know." The CNN reporter asked if he thought the FBI had any new leads in the case.

He said, "I can't tell you detailed information about the case because it is an ongoing investigation."

The reporter asked, "So, do you think this is an individual or a group doing these terrorist bombings in America?"

He replied, "I can't even speculate on that. I don't think we know yet." He did say they were doing the most extensive investigation they could do on all the attacks in America.

Doug knew they didn't have anything on him yet, or they would've had his picture all over the news and looking for him.

The news reporter asked the Liaison what he thought about all the support the "American Terrorist" was getting from people all over America.

He said, "We shouldn't be supporting any terrorist activity in America. We are fighting against terrorism worldwide right now, and we shouldn't tolerate it in America."

She replied, "By the looks of all the protestors and supporters of this individual or group, the people of America think we should start cleaning up our act here at home against the radical Muslim terrorist organizations."

He said, "We have known about many possible sleeper cells in America for years, but we haven't been able to touch them until a plot is uncovered or until they are moved into action by hitting their planned targets.

The "American Terrorist" hit some areas under close security watch by government agencies for some time. Still, we couldn't prove they had weapons and other information until they were exposed. The attacks have allowed the law enforcement agencies to shut down those sites that the American Terrorist attacked."

The reporter said, "Are you saying the "American Terrorist," is a good thing based on that?"

The Liaison just said, "No comment."

When Doug watched the news, he was pleased that he had played a part in shutting down many terrorist camps and other targets he had hit. He was happy the government agencies were shutting the terrorist camps down. He couldn't have asked for a better reward, except for the personal satisfaction of killing the terrorists he was getting for his revenge for Michael's death.

* * *

Chapter 25 - Arkansas

Doug liked how the people in the South rallied behind what he was doing, so he decided to return to the South and hit a few more targets. In Houston, he heard about a suspected training camp near Glenwood, Arkansas. The men who told him about it said they had set up a new training camp near Caddo-Gap, Arkansas. It was not too far from Glenwood in a very remote and beautiful wooded area several miles from town. They said it was so secluded that it was hard to find unless you knew where it was.

Doug would stay at Catherine's Landing RV Park in Hot Springs, Arkansas. It was about a forty-five-minute drive to Glenwood and another forty minutes to the camp. The closer he got to Hot Springs, the more beautiful he thought the Arkansas country was. He soon discovered that Hot Springs are also known as the "Spa City." It is in Garland County and has the most extensive grouping of bathhouses in the United States. The hot springs are the resource for which the area was set aside as the first Federal Recreational Reserve in 1832. (1)

In his opinion, there weren't too many places in America as beautiful as the surrounding area of Hot Springs. He loved all the beautiful trees and lakes and felt this may be America's best-kept secret spot.

Glenwood was the closest city to his next target, located in the Ouachita Mountains. It has approximately two thousand residents and is surrounded by lakes and forests with the beautiful Caddo River flowing through it. The residents are very friendly and like to tell people they don't need a vacation because they enjoy one all year. Some of their recreations include fishing, swimming, and hunting.

Arkansas was the state where the two Army soldiers were shot in Little Rock, and one was killed by an American-born Muslim terrorist who had converted to Islam at age twenty. He was active in radical circles, traveled to the Middle East, and married a Yemeni woman. (24) These were the people that Doug didn't understand. They were born and raised in America and had all the freedoms and liberties we share. They have never lived under the rule of another foreign country, yet they support that country and its radical cause.

After Doug checked into the RV campground, he unhooked his car and headed to Glenwood. He talked to some of the townspeople and asked where the little town of Caddo-O-Gap was located. One of the older men sitting in an old beat-up rocking chair that looked like a hundred years old said, "It's just up yonder a few miles," pointing toward one of the roads leading out of town. He thanked the older man and headed to Caddo-Gap. He soon learned that Caddo-Gap only had a post office, and that was about it.

Once he was there, Doug went into the post office and asked the man at the counter if he knew about some Muslim camp up in the hills. Doug said that some local people from Glenwood told him that a group of Muslims had set up camp about eighteen miles deep in the woods. The man at the counter said, "Take the little dirt road heading east and drive about thirty-five minutes up into the hills, and you'll find it." Doug thanked him and headed up in the direction of the camp.

The narrow dirt road had hickory and pine trees so thick they touched each other at the top from both sides of the road. He felt like he was driving in a tunnel and wondered how the terrorist ever found such a remote and beautiful place. As he made his way up the winding road to the camp, deer and other wild animals were along the road. The camp was so remote they didn't have a guardhouse. They just had a locked four-rail gate on the main road into the camp. As Doug looked around, he saw men dressed in Muslim attire carrying weapons over their shoulders as they strolled around the camp. As soon as they spotted him, they tried to hide their guns. Doug turned his car around and slowly headed back down the mountain.

Now that he knew his next target, he headed back to Hot Springs. That evening, he would dine at the Riverboat Bell of Hot Springs. It was a quiet and relaxing fifteen-mile sunset dinner cruise on Lake Hamilton. The cruise included dinner and entertainment. (1) While on the cruise, he thought this would have been perfect if he had just had his family with him to enjoy it. Without them, the loneliness left him empty and dead inside.

Life no longer had meaning for him except for his mission against the terrorists. He had killed many of the terrorists, which was not satisfying the pain he was feeling inside. He didn't have anyone to share things with, and he missed Shirley telling him everything would be okay. He didn't have Jenifer to call to see how her day went and if there was anything he could do for her. He didn't have Michael to talk to and share his life with. All the loved ones in his life were gone, and all he had to speak to were their ghosts.

The following day, he pulled himself together, put on his mustache, goatee, hat, sunglasses, and a hooded sweatshirt, and drove back to Caddo-O-Gap to visit the terrorist camp. He wanted to observe it with his binoculars and know where everything was located. Once in position, he lay in the grass along the tree line while watching the camp for several hours.

Later that day, on his way down the hill, he saw a young man in a new pickup truck approaching him. As he approached the pick-up, the young man reminded him of Michael. He could see that he was clean-cut with short dark hair and blue eyes as he pulled up next to him. They each rolled down their windows and started a conversation with each other.

The young man looked him over briefly and said, "Hi, how's it going?" Before Doug could answer, he asked, "What are you doing in these parts?"

Doug still hadn't answered his first two questions, so the young man asked him another one, "You have been up at the camp?"

He could tell this young man was anxious to talk about the camp, so he shook his head and said, "I went up to check it out."

The young man said, "Are you part of them?"

Doug laughed, saying, "I'm the furthest thing from those terrorists."

When he said the word terrorist, the young man began to tell Doug how the people in that area were furious that the Muslims had set up a camp in their favorite hunting grounds. I have gone up to the camp and taken potshots into their camp. We like to shake them up and get them excited."

Doug laughed, "How long have they been there?"

The young man said, "They've been there about two years."

He asked the young man what his name was and where he lived.

He told Doug, "My name is Richard Snow, but you can call me Rick." He said that he had been raised in the area his entire life and had his place back down in the holler by Caddo-Gap.

He asked Doug his name and replied, "Charles Fisher, but you can call me Chuck."

They both laughed and reached over and shook hands.

They shut off their cars and sat and talked for about an hour regarding the camp. They talked about how much Rick and his friends hated having it in the hills. He appeared very sincere, reminding Doug of Michael as he talked. After hearing how much Rick and his friends hated having the terrorist camp in their backyards, he felt comfortable talking to him about the camp and its people.

Rick began telling him that he believed about one hundred people in the camp, primarily men. He said they had several SUVs they drove into town to get supplies, and town people would see them from time to time. He and his brother went deer hunting in the area and had a few encounters with men from the camp.

He said, "They heard us shooting our guns, hunted us down, and told us to get out of the area, or there would be problems. We drove toward the camp and were stopped by two men in a black SUV coming from the camp. They questioned us about where we were going and what we were up to."

He told Doug that it angered them so much that he and his brother went to the camp a couple of nights after that incident and shot several rounds in the direction of the camp before speeding away.

He said, "This is our land. We have been here all our lives. It is our home, and they don't have the right to boss us around."

Doug asked him if there was anything else he could tell them about the camp.

He said, "We heard a lot of gunfire and some small explosions on the camp while we have been hunting close to the area.

Doug asked, "Did you ever see the buildings or anything else on the property?"

Rick laughed, "My brother, Todd, and I snuck onto the camp one day to see what was happening. There are several mobile homes and shacks on the camp on about eighty acres."

He said, "They've built about six larger buildings where they conduct some activity."

Doug asked him if they saw any women or children, and he said they didn't see any the day they were there, but they had seen women in the SUVs coming and going from the camp.

Doug asked him, "Do you and your friends want to eliminate this camp?"

Rick's eyes widened, "Are you kidding; we would love to get rid of the camp if we could figure out a way to do it. We have told the local police and other law enforcement agencies about the camp's activities, but nothing ever happened."

Sitting there, talking to Rick, gave Doug an idea.

He told Rick, "I have a proposal for you if you want to hear about it. Can you get your friends together for a meeting so that we can discuss it? You have to tell them this is top secret and classified, and they can't tell anyone, not their friends, girlfriends, wives, or parents."

Rick could tell he was serious as he said, "Sure, when should we all meet?"

Doug told him about the following day at his house around 10:00 am.

Rick said, "That would be great." As he started his engine, he turned his pick-up around, telling Doug to follow him and that he would show him where he lived.

When they drove into the driveway, he saw Rick had a lot of pride in his place. The yard and surrounding area were mowed and cleaned of trash or debris. The house was small and wooden, and he thought maybe just two bedrooms as he pulled up next to it. It was old but well-maintained on several acres. He waived, leaned out his window, and told Rick he would see him tomorrow as he left the driveway.

When Doug got back to his motorhome that night, he thought about it and knew he was taking a big chance involving these young men, but he was looking forward to being with them and seeing if they would perform the way he thought Michael would if he was in that situation.

He was tired of killing the terrorists alone and thought it would be a welcome change to have some company. He didn't need these young men to complete this mission, but he thought it would be a real experience for Rick and the other young men since they wanted to get rid of the camp so severely. It would be interesting to see if they had the guts to do it.

He devised a plan that he thought might work for them and decided to present it to them the next day, but only if he felt comfortable during their first meeting. He had to find out if these young men were just loose cannons or if they were earnest about getting rid of the camp. He also had to find out if he could trust them.

The next day, Doug put on his cap, mustache, and goatee, drove to Caddo- O-Gap, and pulled into Rick's driveway. There were two more pick-up trucks already there besides Rick's.

He cautiously approached the front door, and before he knocked, Rick opened it and said, "Come on in, Chuck, and meet my friends."

When he got close to Rick, he could tell he was about six feet tall with broad shoulders and a thin waist. His dark hair made his eyes stand out even more than he thought when he saw him the day before. Three wide-eyed young men were sitting on a couple of couches and were excited to meet him as he entered. They all appeared to be in their early twenties. Rick introduced his brother Todd, Jason Rockwell, and Kevin Heartland. Jason had bushy blond hair, and it looked like he had just gotten out of bed and put on a baseball cap. He was five feet ten inches tall and about one hundred and eighty pounds, and Doug could tell from his tan face and light eyebrows he spent a lot of time in the sun. Kevin was about the same size as Jason but had shorter dark hair and a baseball cap. He, too, was tanned, and Doug thought he had nice white teeth as he smiled. Todd was just a younger version of Rick with dark hair, but he had brown eyes and was a little thinner. They wore cowboy boots, jeans, and long-sleeved shirts over white tee shirts, and they all smiled as they met Doug. He loved their enthusiasm and energy. These young guys could all be soldiers in Afghanistan right now, some of them dying over there just like Michael had done.

Doug started asking them questions, feeling more comfortable with them, and gradually discussing the Muslim training camp up in the hills. Two boys lived in Glenwood, and Rick's brother lived with his parents in Caddo-O-Gap, far from Rick. The more he talked and listened. He could tell they were sincere about wanting to get rid of the camp. He could hear the anger in their voices as they spoke about how the terrorists had moved into the area and kept everyone away from places they had been going to since they were young to hunt deer, wild pigs, and Turkeys. They weren't just angry with the local authorities but angry that the United States government allowed the camp to be there in the first place.

Doug lied to them and told them he was a retired Special Forces Officer and now a CIA agent. He told them he was there because he was working with the government to find out how to cripple or destroy the Muslim terrorist training camp. The young men all high-fived each other as they listened in eager anticipation. They focused on every word he told them about the Muslim terrorist camp.

He told them he planned to blow up the camp and expose them to the American people and that if they helped, they would each receive ten thousand dollars. He pulled out twenty thousand dollars, put it on the coffee table before them, and said each would get five thousand once they agreed to do the mission. He told them they would get the rest when the mission was completed. He said that the deal would be off if even one word leaked about the mission to anyone. The person who leaked the information would be eliminated. The young men looked at each other when he said that, and they suddenly realized just how serious he was about this mission. It was a bluff on his part, but he knew it would work with them.

He told them to be prepared because many camp members may be killed during this mission.

He said, "You need to look at these terrorists as your enemy. They would kill you and your families if they ever got a chance. They are only targets to you, and you must look at them that way."

He hesitated to see if they would head for the door, but none did.

Rick then asked Doug, "What exactly is the mission, Chuck? Do we have to carry guns and kill people?"

Doug said, "We will go in during the middle of the night while everyone is sleeping and place C-4 bombs and detonators into the main buildings we want to blow up. We don't want to kill the women and children, so we will stay away from homes or buildings where they are located. We want to ensure we blow up their weapons building, our main target. Once we blow it up, there should be several secondary explosions. I have talked to my superiors, and the FBI, CIA, and other law enforcement will shut it down once our mission is complete. We aren't going in with guns; we are going in with explosives to blow them up."

He said that Jason and Kevin would come in from the north side of the camp and place two C-4 bombs on two buildings, while Rick and himself would come up from the south side of the camp and place two C-4 bombs on two more buildings. Todd would wait back at a central location with the van until everyone returned. Doug said he would have the van carry everyone to the camp location from Rick's house, and they would return to Rick's home after completing their mission.

He told the boys he had the C-4 bombs and everything else they needed to complete the mission. All they had to do was show up at Rick's house the night they would hit the compound and be ready to go. He told them to wear all black and paint their faces black so it would be hard to spot them at night. They would hit the targets the next night after he had a chance to study the camp during the day. He would have a sketch of the camp ready. They were to meet him the following evening around 7:00 p.m. at Rick's house.

They all agreed, and as he left, he said, "I will see all of you tomorrow night, and remember, this is classified, so don't say a word to anyone."

The boys were excited to be getting ten thousand dollars for doing something they wanted to do to the Muslim terrorist camp in the first place. They probably would have done it for free, but Doug wanted to make everything "look and feel real" for them.

Doug left them, drove up to the camp, and parked where his car couldn't be seen. He studied the camp for the rest of the day with his binoculars. He crept around to both sides of the camp, so he knew what they would encounter from those sides when they entered the camp. After he was satisfied he had enough information regarding the location of the buildings in the camp, he made his way back to his car and returned to his campsite to rest. Involving these young men would be a massive risk, but he was willing to take one.

The next day, Doug wore his disguise and caught a cab to a local used car dealership in Hot Springs. He had seen a white van on the car lot a few days earlier, so he purchased the van under his fake name and left. Once he had it in his possession, he drove it to a place near his campground and parked it. He waited until late afternoon and then returned to his camp and loaded it with the C-4 bombs, detonators, and phones he had worked on during the day. Once everything was loaded, he drove to a remote area, put on his black clothing with his disguise, and took the additional money he had promised the young men.

When he got to Rick's house that evening, all the young men were hyped and anxious to go. He gave each of them surgical gloves and told them to put them on before they left.

As he handed each pair, he said, "It will keep your fingerprints off anything in the van or on the bombs. We don't want you to be captured because of your DNA."

Doug went over the map with them, so they understood it completely. They were already familiar with the camp and its layout, so it didn't take long to explain where their target buildings were located.

Doug showed them a C-4 bomb and reviewed how it worked. He told them they would turn the phones on when they got to the camp. He kept the extra phone he would use to call the phones on the bombs strapped to his chest with duct tape.

He told the boys, "We will turn off the car lights the last two miles before we get to the camp and find our way to an area I have picked out to hide the Van about three-quarters of a mile from the entrance to the camp. Then, we will walk the rest of the way to the camp's backsides and take up our respective positions. Once we have placed the bombs on our targets, return like you came in, and we will meet back at the van. We will meet up in one hour after you place the bombs. If we aren't back in one hour, we will leave without that person."

He gave Jason a watch at the same time as the one he was wearing and said, "We will place the bombs on the target on or about the same time, so we will each make our approach onto the compound starting at exactly 2:00 a.m." He told the boys not to talk once they were out of the van. The boys were suddenly reticent on the drive up to the camp. Doug figured it was nerves and anticipation. Doug thought Michael must have felt like that when he went out on several missions.

The two teams split up when they hid the van and went to their designated position. Before they left, he turned on the phones attached to the bombs. Once they were in the position, both teams waited until exactly 2:00 a.m. and headed for their targets.

Rick and Doug crept slowly into the compound, keeping very low as they moved. Even though the terrorists had cleared most of the trees' camp, knee-high grass still led to the buildings. Reaching the buildings took about ten minutes, and they could put bombs on their targets without any trouble. As they turned to go back the way they had come in, they heard dogs barking, and huge floodlights came on that lit up the entire area. A few guards came out of the shacks. Just as Doug and Rick were at the edge of the property, shots were being fired in their direction. As they hurried back to the van, they heard more gunshots coming from the camp in the other direction. It was just a few short blasts from an automatic weapon, just like the ones fired at him and Rick. He was hoping Kevin and Jason were okay. He would've felt terrible if one of them was hurt or killed by the terrorists.

Doug and Rick returned to the van and waited ten minutes before Jason and Kevin returned. He rushed everyone into the van, and they headed back down the hill.

On the way down, he asked them what happened back at the camp, and Kevin said, "We had just placed the bombs on the building and heading back when all the lights came on, and we heard gunfire from the camp. A big Rottweiler from the camp came tearing toward us as we started running, and it was on top of us before we knew it. We had to beat it over the head with some large rocks we grabbed on the ground. The noise from the dog's yelps must have alerted the guards to our position, so they shot in our direction as the dog ran back to camp."

Doug said, "Did anyone get hurt?" Kevin looked down at his arm, "I have a few bite marks on my arm, but nothing real serious."

Doug was relieved that none of them had been shot.

After they traveled several miles down the dirt road, Doug had Todd pull the van over to the side, and he said, "You men want to see some fireworks?" He pulled off the phone attached to his chest and turned it on.

They all said, at about the same time, "Hell, yeah."

Doug started dialing the numbers to the phones on the bombs attached to the buildings, and they started going off like a Fourth of July fireworks show. There were also several secondary explosions, so he figured they must have hit their weapons cache. The boys laughed as they all were "high-fiving" each other, yelling and bouncing up and down on the seats.

When they got back to Rick's house, Doug gave each of them the remaining five thousand dollars he had promised them and thanked them for a job well done. He told them, "I couldn't have done it without you, men."

They shook hands as he said, "You men care for yourself. That was a successful mission, and I think the Special Forces soldiers and America would've been very proud of all of you tonight."

The young men shook hands and hugged each other, and he thought, I know Michael would have been proud to have had them on his team. After he left the boys, he drove the van to Hamilton Lake and sank it. He waited until it was entirely out of sight before returning to town. He then caught a cab back to his campground.

When law enforcement arrived at the exploded camp and checked things out in the daylight, they found parts of rifles, grenades, and other metal fragments that had been blown all over the compound from the explosions. The FBI was called to secure the compound where no one else could get hurt from undetonated grenades and ammunition. It was all over the local Arkansas news reporting that a new terrorist training camp near Caddo-O-Gap, Arkansas, had been hit by the "American Terrorist."

The reports said that a lot of people had died from explosions in the camp. They still didn't know how many were killed because they were still sorting through the debris. The report went on to say several explosions and secondary explosions shook the area for miles. The news correspondents expressed some fear and concern that there may be more of these types of camps throughout the United States in hidden areas like this one.

Other news reports focused on the threat radicals pose to the United States military. The recent arrests of a former United States Army soldier for supporting a Muslim terrorist group in Maryland and a Muslim arrested for conspiring to attack military troops in Tampa, Florida, demonstrated the extent of the problems associated with Muslim terrorists. (11) The more Doug heard about this activity, the more he knew he was doing the right thing for America.

* * *

Chapter 26 - Alabama

Doug loved the history of Alabama. It's where the Civil Rights movement started back in 1955 when Rosa Parks, an African American from Montgomery, Alabama, was ordered to go to the back of the bus where all the blacks were supposed to sit while the whites sat in the front. That day, she refused to go to the back of the bus, and her much-publicized actions led to the Civil Rights Movement. On this mission, he would stay in Montgomery and visit the historic Rosa Parks Museum.

Doug checked into an RV Park just outside of town and set up his campsite to plan his next attack. The following day, he got up, went to the Museum, and saw the bus Rosa Parks rode on that famous day in history. He spent the entire day going through the museum and to other historical sites in Alabama.

Doug's target in Alabama was a Muslim terrorist training camp called "Fox Den." It was a camp hidden in the woods near Toby's junction, about twenty miles from town. He loved how the Southern people had rallied behind some of his previous attacks in Arkansas, Georgia, and Tennessee. He hoped to gather even more support when he exposed the "Fox Den" terrorist camp. While on his tours, he asked the tour guides and other local people about the camp's location. He wasn't surprised he could get a general idea of the camp because everyone he talked to seemed agitated that it was right in their backyards.

The following day, he got up early and headed toward the camp. After driving a few hours, he located at the end of a long, winding dirt road. As he approached the camp entrance, he saw the familiar guardhouse like the ones he had seen at several of the other locations. The guard on duty stopped him and asked him what he wanted. He told him he must have gotten lost while looking for a relative's house and was trying to find his way back to town. The guard raised his eyebrows and cocked his head to one side, and said, "Just go back down the way you came, and you'll run into the main road in about twenty miles."

Doug sat a little higher in his seat and looked around the camp. He asked, "What kind of place is this?

The guard wasn't very friendly and replied, "It is a Muslim religious retreat."

Doug then knew he was at the right place because no religious camp needed a guard at the entrance. He thanked the guard and asked him where he could turn around. The guard pointed and said for him to back up, make a U-turn in the road, and go back the way he came. On returning to town, he planned his next move to blow up the camp. That night, while back at his campsite, he formulated a plan.

The next day, he walked into town, rented a car under a fake name, drove back to his campsite, and parked it in the visitor section. He took two C-4 bombs, wrapped them with duct tape, attached a phone to them, and stuck them and his Muslim disguise in a brown paper bag next to him on the passenger-side floorboard. He also made sure he had an extra phone with him. He taped his loaded pistol and a whole extra clip to the inside of his left leg. He went to a local hardware store and purchased an air pump. He stopped and put on his Muslim disguise to the "Fox Den" camp.

When Doug got within a few miles of the camp's main entrance, he pulled over, let the air out of his left-back tire, and raised the trunk lid. He waited for a car with a lone driver heading toward the camp to get close, then jumped out of his car and waved him over. He told the driver he had a flat tire and didn't know how to fix it. He asked the driver if he knew how to change a tire and told him he would give him twenty dollars if he would change it. The driver said he would fix it with a spare tire in the trunk. Doug shrugged and said, "I don't know if there is one; it's a rental."

The driver exited, went to Doug's car, and looked in the trunk. He found the spare tire and put the jack under the car's frame to change the tire. While the driver was changing the tire, Doug took the brown bag with the C-4 from his floorboard and walked to the driver's car. He ensured the driver was busy as he opened the door to the driver's car and put the bag under the passenger seat. He planned to have the driver deliver the bomb into the camp for him. Once he was in camp, Doug would blow it up.

After the driver had the tire changed, Doug started to hand him a twenty-dollar bill and thanked him for his trouble. As the driver reached out to take the money, he looked at Doug funny. He quickly turned and ran to his car. That's when Doug realized his disguise had gotten wet from the sweat on his face and had parts falling off. The driver retrieved a pistol from his car, and before Doug could get back into his vehicle, the driver had him lie face down on the ground. He pointed the pistol at his head and asked, "Why are you wearing a disguise? Do you have something to hide?" Doug didn't say anything; he just lay on the dirt road and contemplated his next move.

After a few minutes, the driver told him to get up because he would take him to the camp leader and determine what he wanted to do with him. As Doug stood up, he raised his arms halfway in the air and held them that way until he got in on the passenger side of the driver's car. Once the driver believed he was sitting securely, he closed the door behind Doug. He quickly started to get in from the driver's side. The entire time, he had his pistol aimed at Doug's head.

Doug reached down and pulled out his pistol without moving his head or body during that short moment. As the driver started to sit down in the seat next to him, Doug shot him in the side of the head. He thought that dummy should have tied me up before he put me in his car or, at the very least, checked me for weapons.

Doug grabbed the C-4 bag from under the seat and ran to his car. He turned around and headed down toward town as fast as he could. When he got about twelve miles down the road, a black SUV came quickly toward him. As it got closer, it slowed down and stopped in the middle of the road as if to not let Doug pass. When he got within about twenty yards of it, he stopped his car as two men jumped out of the SUV with automatic weapons and started coming toward it. Doug figured they must be guards positioned somewhere near the dirt road entrance, and they monitor everyone that goes to and from the camp. Someone from the camp must have notified them of the driver he had just killed.

He didn't say anything as they approached. He immediately rolled down his window, grabbed his pistol, and shot the guard closest to his car in the chest. The other one started firing his automatic weapon into Doug's car. He ducked and quickly opened the door on the passenger side, rolled out, and took cover behind his car. Glass and bullets were flying everywhere as the shooter continued to shoot at the vehicle. It was the first time he had ever been in an actual gun battle at close range. He fired over the top of the car in the guard's direction until his clip was empty and reloaded. He knew he didn't have much time to think about things; he just had to follow his instincts to help him survive.

He hid behind the car and thought, "Keep your cool, Doug; don't lose your head and do something crazy. Think about what you need to do next." He waited until the shooter emptied his bullet clip and started running to get behind the SUV to reload his weapon. That's when Doug took a quick aim and shot him in the back before he made it to the vehicle's cover. Once he was down, Doug crept slowly over to him. He was still squirming around on the ground, so Doug put another bullet in his head. He then went to the guard he had shot earlier and put another shot in his head to make sure he was dead.

Doug's rental car had a flat tire and bullet holes all over the driver's side of the vehicle. Most of the windows had been blown out, so he knew he couldn't drive it back to town in that condition. He grabbed the phone from the seat and ran to the SUV. He ensured the keys were in it, and no one else was around as he jumped in. He quickly turned it around in the middle of the road and headed back toward town. His heart was pumping a million miles a minute, and he breathed heavily from all the excitement. Sweat started to roll down the side of his nose from his forehead. He wiped the sweat with his shirt sleeve and thought, "Wow! That was close; I could've bit the dust. I think I'm getting too old for this crap."

He waited a few minutes, then called the phone number attached to the C-4 bomb still in the rented car. He heard the explosion in the distance as he continued into town. On his way down the dirt road, he passed another vehicle speeding toward the camp. He ducked down so the driver couldn't see who was driving and waved with his left hand as they passed. He knew he had to get into town soon, or the camp people would trap him and be in another gun battle. It was just a matter of time before they would be all over him. The one thing he feared most about those small dirt roads was being trapped along the way. After a few minutes, he looked in his rear-view mirror, and the guy he had passed a few minutes earlier was coming up fast behind him.

Then, the chase began down the narrow dirt road. Doug was hogging the entire road, so the driver couldn't pass and was right on his bumper. He knew he had to do something before getting into town, so he sped up the SUV as fast as he could safely. He stuck his pistol in his belt, and when he was sure about twenty to thirty yards were separating him and the driver behind him, he braced himself with both hands on the steering wheel and slammed on the brakes. The SUV came to a sliding stop, and the driver behind him came plowing into the back of the SUV at full speed. Doug jumped out with his pistol and ran to the car behind him.

The driver was still trying to figure out what had just happened as Doug approached the car, shot him through the window, and killed him before he could get out of the vehicle. Doug then ran back to the SUV and headed down the road toward town once again. On the way into town, he thought, "I hope there aren't any more surprises. I've had enough fun for one day." After much anxiety and anticipation, he finally made it into town without further confrontations or obstacles. Once there, he released a massive sigh of relief as he fixed his Muslim disguise and abandoned the crunched SUV in an alley between two large buildings. He walked to where he could catch a taxi and had the driver drop him off about a mile from his RV camp. He walked the rest of the way to his campsite.

He removed the Muslim disguise before Doug returned to camp and stuck it inside his shirt. Once back at his campsite, he carefully packed everything in the motor home and left within an hour. He wasn't sure where he was going; he just wanted to get out of there as fast as possible. He believed the people from the camp and law enforcement would search for someone all over town once they found the SUV.

While driving east, he had time to reflect as he said, "Man, you got lucky this time, Doug." He realized how he very narrowly escaped from the driver that changed his tire. He knew he would never have escaped if the driver hadn't been so rattled or in a hurry to return him to the camp's leader. He knew that once the Muslims had their hands on him, they would have tortured and killed him or, even worse, turned him over to law enforcement.

The next day, the news reported that four armed Muslim men had been killed, and a car had been blown up along the dirt road leading to the "Fox Den" camp. The news reported that the attack fit the method of operation of the "American Terrorist." The people in Alabama were agitated and protesting in the streets about the camp. They were angry that the Muslims had armed guards, and it was so close to their homes. They had been trying to get law enforcement to do something about the camp for a long time. Doug needed it, especially after his close encounters with being captured, the gun battle, and the chase with the armed shooters. As he drove along, he thought, "Well, Michael, I got the attention of law enforcement and, in the process, killed four more of the terrorists."

The closer he got to Florida, he started thinking about possible targets. He knew Florida had many suspected terrorist cells hiding in a lot of different locations, so he just had to find them. He knew it would be risky for him because of all the law enforcement security in Florida, but he had to take a chance.

Doug was tired of moving from place to place, setting up his campground, taking it down, and always hiding in seclusion. He never really knew just how safe he was or when the law enforcement people would catch him. He had so many close calls during his mission that he believed they would eventually get him. He was also getting tired of all the planning and killing. He was starting to feel that he was feeling some vindication for Michael's death since he had killed so many terrorists.

* * *

Chapter 27 - Florida

Doug had never been to Disney World in Orlando, Florida, although he had taken Michael to Disneyland in Los Angeles several times. He decided to stay in the town of Kissimmee at an RV Park called Paradise Park. It had everything he needed to set up his motor home and relax for several days. After he arrived, he unhooked his car and had everything situated on the campsite before he headed into town to check things out.

He wasn't wasting any time; he wanted to find out what his next target would be. He went to a secluded area, put on his Muslim disguise, and continued his drive to one of the local mosques. Once there, he strolled up to the door and went inside. Even though he had a bad experience with his disguise on the last mission, he had become very comfortable with his disguise and felt he fit right in with everyone else. He just had to ensure he had everything attached right before joining them. A few people were inside, so he approached one of them and asked him in Arabic when they would have a meeting he could attend. The man told him they had a meeting daily at around 7:00 pm. He thanked him and said he would return when the meeting started.

Doug spent the next few hours just walking around the streets as he had done in Seattle. He approached him when he saw a man who looked like he might be of Middle Eastern nationality. The man understood and spoke Arabic. He asked about the Muslim community and where they gathered besides the mosques. Doug then asked him if there was a safe house where some Muslims against the Jews gathered.

The man was a little reluctant to give him any information, so he pulled a few twenty-dollar bills, held them toward him, and said, "I need a safe place to stay for a few days. I just came from Kabul."

The man reached out, took the money, looked around, and whispered, "Go about seven miles south near the outskirts of town, and you will come to Carney Road. When you get on Carney Road, go east a few miles, and there is a big white house with a white fence around it. When you get to the gate, tell the guard on duty the words, "Allah is Supreme," and they will let you in."

Doug thanked him and returned to the mosque where he had been earlier.

He spent about an hour in the mosque with the women and children, and he could tell this mosque wasn't preaching about destroying Israel and the Christians. Satisfied there was no terrorist activity, he drove to the house on Carney Road to check it out. When he got to the house, it was already dark outside. The house was an enormous two-story, sprawling, multi-level roofed house. A white-painted concrete wall about eight feet tall, rounded at the top, surrounded the entire property. It had a beautiful double wrought-iron gate that opened into a drive that led to a huge circle driveway with a lion fountain in the middle. The grounds were well maintained, and he estimated at least five acres encompassing the property. The house had a lot of outside lights and was completely lit up.

He thought this must be the place of some essential Muslim leader of one of the large mosques. When he saw the guard at the gate, he knew he must be at the right place. Doug knew he had a weapon nearby, even if the guard didn't appear armed. Once convinced he had the right place, he drove back to his campground for a good night's sleep.

The following day, he spent most of his time being a tourist and walking the Disney World grounds. Even though it was beautiful, it was a sad day for him; everywhere he looked in his mind, he saw Michael running around and having fun like he used to do when he was a little boy. He missed Michael, and being there just magnified his pain.

On the way back to his campground later that day, the pain turned into anger, and once again, he was ready to go after the radical Muslim terrorist organization that had killed Michael. He didn't sleep much that night; he kept tossing, turning, and thinking about the terrorists and Michael. It kept running through his mind what Michael could have possibly gone through as he took his last breath.

The following day, Doug left the campground before daylight, dressed in his Muslim disguise and carrying a bag with a few things inside, including his prayer rug and the Qur'an. Once off the campground, he called a cab to take him to the house on Carney Road. He left his car and everything else in the camp locked up because he wasn't sure how long he would be gone. When he arrived at the house on Carney Road, he walked up to the gate and said to the guard, "Allah is Supreme." The guard looked at him to see if he had a weapon and opened the gate.

Once inside the gate, he searched Doug and his bag for weapons before letting him go further.

He asked him what he wanted, and Doug told him, "I'm from Kabul, and I heard this is a place I could stay for a few days while I'm passing through." The guard motioned for him to go to the house.

He had the Qur'an and prayer rug when he got to the house. He was greeted coldly by an armed guard at the door as he motioned for Doug to come in. He removed his shoes, glanced around, and saw three or four other men armed. He spoke Arabic to the guard and said, "I was told I might be able to stay here a few days before I continue my journey.

I just came from Kabul and am heading to "Islamcity" from here." The guard didn't say a word as he motioned for Doug to stay there. He entered another room, and soon, a beautiful young Middle Eastern woman came into the space behind the guard wearing a Hijab. He gave her greetings, and she started asking him questions about how he had gotten to Florida. He told her about how he had come from Kabul. He said he paid a lot of money to be smuggled in from offshore in Florida.

After she had asked him several other questions and was satisfied with his answers, she had one of the guards escort him to a big, open room. The room had about ten or twelve single-bed mattresses on the floor. All lined a few feet apart on each side of the room. Eight or nine men were sleeping or relaxing on the mattresses. They didn't pay much attention to Doug as he picked out one of the beds and thanked the guard. He laid out his prayer rug and pretended to go through the prayer to Allah before he lay down.

He spent most of the next day just keeping to himself. Early afternoon, a girl brought in a rolling table with food. She quickly left, and all the men went to the table and helped themselves. He was getting hungry, so he joined in. While getting his food, Doug overheard a couple of men whispering about a target they would hit soon. He couldn't quite make out what they were saying, and they didn't trust him enough to talk aloud. He pretended he wasn't interested in what they were talking about and turned and walked away. He was in the room for two nights, the only room he was allowed in besides a large bathroom down the hall. Some guards watched his every move. When he went to the bathroom down the hallway, he saw a couple more rooms like the one he was in with mattresses filled with men. He soon realized these people were part of a terrorist plot that was going to take place soon. It was the terrorist group that he was looking, hoping to find. He couldn't determine their target but knew it had to be something big.

Late afternoon of the third day, he told the guards he was ready to leave. He thanked them for letting him stay and left the house. As he left, he checked the house for the most vulnerable spot to hit it with a vehicle. Just left of the main entrance, there was an open courtyard in the middle of the house, and he figured if it were hit from that spot with explosives, it would destroy the entire house.

Once he left the compound, he called a cab and returned to his campsite to plan his strategy. He knew he had to get onto the compound with his bombs and destroy the house before carrying out their big attack.

Doug had been thinking about it and decided this would be the last attack on Muslim terrorist targets. He had grown weary of all the killings, traveling, hiding, and feeling like a fugitive. He missed his family, and nothing he did would bring them back. Going to Disney World made him realize he would never get used to being alone. His family was no longer with him, and he yearned to be with them again. He figured the best way to accomplish that goal was to go on a suicide mission of his own. He knew that because of all his close encounters and the mistakes he had made, eventually, he would slip up, and law enforcement would catch him. He didn't want to be captured and have the news media parade him around and make a spectacle out of him. He also knew there was no way he would spend the rest of his life in prison if there was any way he could prevent it.

That night, he sat down and wrote a letter that he was going to send to all the major television networks that he wanted the American people to see and hear, and this is what it said:

My name is Douglas James Cotton, and I'm from Visalia, California. I'm a retired doctor who spent thirty years caring for people and saving lives. I served honorably in the United States Army as a sniper during the Vietnam War in 1968. My grandson's name is Michael Douglas Hunter, and he was a Special Forces soldier killed by a radical Muslim terrorist insurgent, I.E.D. (Improvised Explosive Device). He was killed in Afghanistan on December 2, 2009, while serving his tour of duty. That is the reason I hate all Muslim terrorist organizations. My goal during the attacks on the terrorist organizations in America was to avenge Michael's death. I declared war on the thirty-five terrorist cells and camps in America. I intended to find them, expose them to the people and the United States government, and destroy them. I acted alone during my attacks and was not part of any organization or conspiracy. The radical Muslim terrorists should not be allowed to use our constitution's freedom of speech and assembly to hide their true intentions of destroying Israel and the West. It is your country, and you must always protect it from being free. Don't let another foreign organization dictate how you live in America.

As my last will, I would like you to use half of the money from my remaining assets to start a memorial in Washington, D.C., for the soldiers who have died in Iraq and Afghanistan and the other half for The Disabled American Veterans. I love you, America, and God bless you.

Douglas James Cotton

The next day, Doug went to a Kinko's, made copies of this letter, and mailed a copy of it to CNN News, Fox News, CBS, and ABC News stations. They would have their documents in a few days, and everyone would finally know the truth about the "American Terrorist" and who he was. He boxed up the cash and all his valuable items left in the motor home and put them in a box along with a letter to Randy saying, "I love you, brother, take care of your family." He set the box up for FedEx and overnight delivery so that Randy would have it.

That afternoon, he spent his time attaching wires to the remaining I.E.D. s he had left, putting detonators in the remaining C-4 blocks, and getting everything ready for his final attack. He moved the bombs to the front of the motor home once they were all set up and ready to go. He took his rifle and everything under the back seat of his car and put it in the motor home, along with the remaining rounds of ammunition. He parked his car in the RV visitor parking lot with a letter inside that said to contact Randy Cotton with his address and phone number. Doug had the Mercedes' ownership changed to Randy a few days earlier and put Randy's keys in the FedEx box in the car's back seat. He figured the car would probably be confiscated once they found out it was the car used by "The American Terrorist."

After dark, Doug took a large stick of the C-4 and drove to the house on Carney Road, parked down the street and away from the gate. He snuck up to the guard location and placed the C-4, with a phone detonator attached, outside the wall where it couldn't be seen. He drove back to the campground and had some of his favorite red wine as he prepared his mind to hit his last target. Before he went to bed that night, he got down on his hands and knees and said another prayer for God to forgive him for killing innocent children. He also said an individual prayer to Shirley, Jenifer, and Michael.

The next day, just before he pulled out of the campsite in his motor home, he ensured he had the remote-control detonator strapped to his chest and a phone in his lap. While driving to his final target, he told Shirley, Jennifer, and Michael how much he loved them and hoped to see them soon. Just before he arrived at the gate to his target, he stopped and ensured no cars were heading in his direction.

His heart was beating rapidly, and he was anxious and nervous as he dialed the number on the bomb at the guard gate. When it blew up, it blew a large hole in the wall and sent the gates and pieces of concrete flying in the air. Parts of the debris landed on his motor home as he pushed the gas pedal to the floor and drove as fast as it would go down the drive and straight toward the courtyard and the middle of the big house.

Armed guards started pouring out of the house after they heard the explosion at the front gate, and they were taking shots at Doug as he ducked down in the seat. He crashed head-on into the house at full speed, and he pushed the button to the detonator at the same time as the motor home plunged into the house. The explosion was so large that it destroyed most of the houses destroyed by the initial blast. There were also several secondary explosions inside, destroying what was left of the big house. Bullets from the left-over ammunition kept firing the rest of the day and into the night. Several hours before the fire department or law enforcement agencies could get near the house.

A few days later, it seemed the only thing on the news was about Doug's last target and how "The American Terrorist" had foiled another massive attack planned against America. It was reported that the radical Muslim terrorist organization had plans to blow up and kill thousands of people at Walt Disney World in Orlando, Florida. The terrorists all worked as or for vendors that provided services in Walt Disney World. They had full and easy access to Walt Disney World without being searched. They had plans to infiltrate the park with over forty fellow Muslim terrorists wearing suicide vests to blow up thousands of men, women, and children. The bombings were to take place simultaneously while the people were enjoying the evening fireworks show at the end of the day. It would have made the attacks on the World Trade Center seem small in comparison.

His last attack was successful as he foiled one of the most significant planned attacks on American soil. He had killed forty-three people in the safe house and wounded four others. Among them were two of the top Muslim radical terrorist leaders of a large terrorist organization. One was on America's top ten Most Wanted terrorist lists, and a female killed was also on the government's "terrorist watch" list.

A few days later, one of the commentators read what a government official had anonymously written about Doug on Good Morning America. It said: "It had to take a retired doctor and grieving grandfather who was sworn to uphold the Hippocratic Oath to open up the American public's eyes and expose the terrorist organizations already here in America.

One man's struggle for revenge against the terrorist organizations for killing his grandson in Afghanistan showed the American people there is evil lurking at home in our backyards. He played a significant role in finding them, exposing them, and stopping many attacks before they happened.

We could never call a terrorist a hero in America, but I want to say thank you, "American Terrorist," for everything you did for my family and me."

The government agencies were now on the right track to shutting down all the suspected terrorist training camps and gathering places in the United States. They were no longer going to let any terrorist organizations come to America and impose their will on the American people through fear and intimidation. No longer were they going to be able to use our constitutional freedoms as protection to spread their lies and hatred. The people of America weren't going to sit back and let a foreign country or organization dictate policy or take over America without a fight.

* * *

Author's notes

This book and its characters are fictional and not intended to represent the truth.

Being a father and a grandfather to a military-age son and grandson, I thought about how I would react or feel if I lost my son or grandson in a war like Iraq or Afghanistan. Not knowing what that would feel like, I can only imagine my extreme pain, anger, and frustration. The thought of a loss like that inspired me to write this book. I would never be able to carry out my fantasy or desire to destroy the terrorist or their organizations if something like that happened to me, but I would probably want to deep in my heart. Most of this book is about Doug hunting down and destroying the suspected Terrorist Organizations in America because he wanted revenge for killing his grandson.

I would never recommend or advocate this type of violence against the Muslim people or any other group or organization in America. I would never say to someone that they should take the law into their own hands. Most of the Muslim people in America are American Citizens who were born and raised here. They love America just as much as the Christians, Catholics, Buddhists, Jewish people, and other religious people of America. Most Muslims in America are peaceful and loving people who do not align themselves with hatred like radical terrorist organizations. Like most races and religions, a tiny number of extremists always cause problems for the rest of their people.

The United States government has spent billions of taxpayers' dollars trying to keep America safe from terrorist attacks since September 11, 2001. Although there have been over eighty attacks on American Citizens since 2001, I think the FBI, CIA, Homeland Security, and other law enforcement agencies have done an excellent job of foiling the major terrorist plots against America before they happen. I commend them for doing an excellent job of keeping America safe. We should all pray that their diligent efforts will continue to succeed.

* * *

A Grandfather's Promise – poem

You, terrorists, have spread your fear throughout the land
    And made men tremble in fear, all from your hand
    In the name of "Allah," and that's what you believe
    Why are all you terrorists so naïve
    Why do you hide behind the Qur'an to fit your own needs
    Spreading fear and hatred, with all your dirty deeds
    The Qur'an doesn't say to kill Christians and Jew
    You extremists twisted it to fit your point of view
    You should never have killed my most precious grandson
    You'll find your time on Earth is all but done
    I'll hunt you down in the little camps where you hide
    You're nothing but cowards with unjustified pride
    You've created the I.E.D. bombs to kill and maim
    I'll find you and kill you at your own game
    You'll be crying for mercy when I hunt you down
    Hoping that somewhere, you have a crown
    I'll blow you to pieces by the time I'm through
    Praying to Allah, that's my promise to you

* * *

Sources of Information

1. Wikipedia, the free encyclopedia

2. Terroristplanet.com "(Your online Terrorist and World Treats Magazine)" 1/11/2010

3. One Man's War on Terror by Zachary Block-Brown Alumni Magazine November/December 2002 - Steven Emerson in the News.

4. Are Terrorist Cells Targeting America by Steven Emerson - Author of the documentary film "Jihad in America-http://www.steveemerson.com/4267/one-mans-war-on-terror

5. Al-Qaeda - Osama bin Laden's Network of Terror by Laura Hayes, Borgna Brunner and Beth Rowen http://www.infoplease.com/spot/al-qaeda terrorism.html[1]

6. Islam - Wikipedia, the free encyclopedia - 12/22/2011

7. Indianapolis, Martial Law Drills, conducted by DHS and FBI KnowtheLies.com - 1/12/2012

8. Army Special Forces Overview - Military Fitness Military.com http://www.military.com/military-fitness/army-special-operations - 12/27/2011

9. Special Forces Training/Go Army Http: goarmy.com/soldier-life/being-asoldier/ongoingtraining/specialized-schools[2] - 12/24/2012

10. Soft jihad in America's schools (oneNewsNow.com by Karen Gushta: -

---

1.   http://www.infoplease.com/spot/al-qaeda%20terrorism.html

2.   http://www.goarmy.com/soldier-life/being-asoldier/ongoingtraining/specialized-schools

3/18/2011

11. American Jihadist Terrorism: Combating a Complex Threat by Jerome P.

Bjelopera

(Specialist in Organized Crime and Terrorism) - 11/15/2011

12. In Afghanistan, special units do dirty work USATODAY.com - 12/29/2011

13. Al-Qaeda—Infoplease.com - 12/10/2011

14. Breastcancer.org (stages of breast Cancer) - 12/13/2011

15. The Christian Science Monitor (A soldier's life in Afghanistan)

16. U.S. Terror Cells 101 (The Patriotic Resistance Movement) http://www.radiojihad.org/U.S.php - 1/4/212[3]

17. Hamas terrorists took a blood oath to kill http://wwwIsraelsMessiah.com/terrorism/hamas.html12/31/2011

18. The Long War Journal (Taliban attack Afghan Army bases in Kabul, Kunduz by Bill Roggio -12/19/2010

19. Ohio woman sentenced for aiding terrorist group http://wwwInfidelsarecool.com/2011/06/Ohiowomansentenced-for-aiding-terrorist-group/ - 1/12/2012[4]

20. L115A3 Long Range Rifle - British Army Website http://wwwArmy.mod.uk/equipment/supportweapons/1459.aspx - 12/25/2011

21. Recreational Shooting, Barstow Field Office, Bureau LandManagemenCalifornia http://www.blm.gov/ca/st/en/fo/Barstow - 12/28/2011

22. Terrorist Cells Training Camps in America - actual Video provided by the Christian Action Network - Christianaction.org - 2/19/2009

23. The Heritage Foundation - leadership for America U.S. Thwarts

19

---

3.   http://www.radiojihad.org/U.S.php%20-%201/4/212

4.   http://wwwInfidelsarecool.com/2011/06/Ohiowomansentenced-for-aiding-terrorist-group/%20-%20%20%20%20%20%20%20%20%20%20%20%20%20%20%20%20%20%20%20%201/12/2012

Terrorist Attacks

against America since 9/11 by James Jay Carafano, Ph.D. 11/13/ 2007

24. Tennessee Trained American Jihadist Guns Down

Two Soldiers in Little Rock - conservative crusader.com - 12/9/ 2011

23, Osama bin Laden - Wikipedia - the free Encyclopedia

* * *

Disclaimer

This book references some actual events; however, it has been fictionalized, and all persons appearing in it are fiction. Any resemblance to real people, living or dead, is entirely coincidental.

* * *

Special Thanks

I want to thank my daughter, Danielle Nicole Derby Carter, for helping me with all the computer work on this book. She also assisted in the cover design.

I want to thank my wife, Tami, who inspired and encouraged me to write this book.

I want to thank my sister, Sharon Duvall, for giving me ideas and suggestions for the book. I am genuinely grateful for her help.

Other books by Ron L. Carter

Fiction -American Terrorist – The Revenge Continues
    Fiction - American Terrorist – Silent Killer
    Nonfiction - Twenty-One Months
    Fiction - From the Darkness of My Mind
    Fiction – Unearthly Realms
    Fiction – Night Crawlers
    Fiction - Night Crawlers – Reign of Terror
    Fiction – Nightcrawlers – The Nightmares Continue
    Fiction - In Defense of Mankind

Fiction - Accidental Soldiers
Fiction - Ignited
Fiction - Zak Thomas – The Monster Hunter
Fiction - Lost Waters
Love me now, don't wait - Poetry

www.ingramcontent.com/pod-product-compliance
Lightning Source LLC
Chambersburg PA
CBHW060545160726
47991CB00001B/443